ARDOR

or How would-be Nobel Prize winner C. Milosz enjoyed the high life with low life in Italy, hobnobbed with a Viktor Yanukovych look-alike, and met his Muse on the rooftop of the Duomo

ALEXANDER J. MOTYL

ANAPHORA LITERARY PRESS

Augusta, Georgia

ANAPHORA LITERARY PRESS
2419 Southdale Drive
Hephzibah, GA 30815
http://anaphoraliterary.com

Book design by Anna Faktorovich, Ph.D.

Printed in the United States of America, United Kingdom and in Australia on acid-free paper.

Published in 2016 by Anaphora Literary Press

Alexander J. Motyl—1st edition.

Library of Congress Control Number: 2016904783

Library Cataloging Information

Motyl, Alexander J., [October 21, 1953] author.
ARDOR : or how would-be Nobel Prize winner C. Milosz enjoyed the high life with low life in Italy, hobnobbed with a Viktor Yanukovych look-alike, and met his Muse on the rooftop of the Duomo / Alexander J. Motyl
130 p. ; 9 in.
ISBN 978-1-68114-243-2 (softcover : alk. paper)
ISBN 978-1-68114-244-9 (hardcover : alk. paper)
ISBN 978-1-68114-254-8 (ebook)
1. Fiction—Literary. 2. Fiction—Action & Adventure.
3. Fiction—Humorous. I. Title.
PS370-380: American: Prose Fiction.
817: American humor & satire in English.

ARDOR

or How would-be Nobel Prize winner C. Milosz enjoyed the high life with low life in Italy, hobnobbed with a Viktor Yanukovych look-alike, and met his Muse on the rooftop of the Duomo

To Norman and Eva
with affection

New York

ALEXANDER J. MOTYL

ONE

C. Milosz gets invited to a high-powered gathering of movers and shakers, decides to go in the hope of overcoming his writer's block and winning the Nobel Prize, and encounters Fate in the form of the Underwear Incident

If it hadn't been for the Underwear Incident, I might not have had a foreboding about the gathering. Don't get me wrong. Forebodings have never impressed me, either as genuine sensations or literary devices. They're no big deal. They're just indeterminate inklings, inchoate clues, and hazy hints. They may mean something; they may mean nothing. Like most of life, come to think of it. And yet, how can poets ignore forebodings? They cannot, precisely because both poets and forebodings occupy the netherworld between love and logic, clarity and ambiguity, words and signs. Besides, who knows how my life would have unfolded if not for the Underwear Incident?

I know and you know that I've just emerged—unscathed, I add, and with no small hubris—from the logical thickets of a counterfactual. I think I read somewhere that drawing conclusions from false premises presupposes more than it demonstrates, even though the form of counterfactuals has the salutary effect of creating the decidedly false, though not inconvenient, impression that they demonstrate more than they presuppose. But there really is no other way for me to express the subjectively nervous anticipation I felt that day (that gorgeous, sunny day) on the one hand and the objectively opaque circumstances I faced (foreign country, foreign people, foreign tongues) on the other. Is that clear? Probably not. Life never is, and, if it were, it probably wouldn't be worth living. The point is this. I came to Ardor Haus with certain expectations (call them exorbitant or exalted or anything else). And the Underwear Incident rattled them. I'll explain a bit later why I keep referring to this event as an incident, a choice of words you'd be right to assume entails a conscious effort on my part to create the impression (or is it illusion?) of portentousness. As you may have guessed by now, I shall be making parenthetical remarks about my choice of words throughout the text. (If self-reflexivity bothers you, too bad. It's the future, so get used to it.)

In retrospect, everything can be made to look important, to appear to herald the future that came or would have come anyway and that only appears to be inevitable or just plain worthy of attention because it's been tacked on to an event—pardon, an *incident*—that seems to have borne it in its womb. That indirect reference to pregnancy is a godawful image that smells of tawdry Marxian inspiration and the old hairy goat's loopy insistence that crazy revolutionaries can actually hasten the birth pangs of history, as if, for Chrissakes, history were some bloated woman waddling in penguin-like fashion through time. But I can't think of anything better and, besides, it (the image, of course) is precisely the one I'd like to use anyway and, goddammit, will, regardless of what you or anybody else may think about it.

After all, I'm entitled to say and write and think what I will and to say and write and think how I want to, when I want to, and where I want to, because I am, as you may have guessed by now from the rather broad hints in the preceding paragraphs, a writer or more exactly a poet and, even though modern culture holds neither of these vocations in especially high esteem—oh, how I sometimes yearn for the golden age of the Romantics!—I don't care. I am who I am, as Yahweh reportedly told Moses, and just as there was little ole Mose could do about it then, so too there's little you, or anybody else for that matter, can do about it now. So grin and bear it and listen to what I have to say. You may learn a thing or two—which can't possibly be a bad thing, considering the parlous state of education in this great country of ours.

Poets are bards, prophets, seers, troubadours, minstrels, and visionaries. We are the philosopher kings of Plato, even if he had the bad judgment to consign us to caves, where, as far as I can tell, we'd be forever doomed to carry pots and vases before that damned fire, cast shadows on some wall, and watch those buffoons—that's you, buster—squirm in their seats and mistake the shadows for the real thing. Plato, clearly, knew nothing about poets, because if he did, he would've known that, given our propensity for day dreaming and night drinking, we'd stumble and fall and drop those precious clay pots and ceramic vases and, before you could say philosophy rules, we'd have broken all the crockery in the cave. The tied and bound half-wits waiting for the dancing shadows would see nothing but the light of the fire and conclude that light was the only true reality, which was the whole point of the parable. Then they'd just lean back and figure there was no reason to climb out of the cave and raise their mousy eyes to the sun, since the fire was bright enough anyway. That's the thing about us poets. We know more than we think we know and less than others think we don't know.

I wouldn't be surprised if you'd originally guessed I was a philosopher: the reference to counterfactuals couldn't have failed to send you down the wrong evidentiary track (ask yourself: purposely or accidentally?). I am, of course, though only of the amateur variety. I dabble in the classics. I've read an existentialist or two. I've waded through some of Wittgenstein and much of Sartre (well, only his fiction). I can't make heads or tails of Heidegger and Derrida—but I know how to spell and pronounce their names, which you probably can't—and I'm conversant in the differences between the analytic school, the continental school, and the postmodernist school, though I couldn't name any of the folks associated with these schools, even if you put a gun to my head and ordered me to choose between being and nothingness. So what? I am not a namedropper: never was, never will be. I confess to never having tried my hand at philosophy, but it permeates everything I do and say and write: after all, what is poetry if not the quintessence of philosophy? Poets use words to attain truths, essences. Philosophers also use words, though far less successfully. Our truths are eternal; theirs are ephemeral. No wonder they give Nobel Prizes to poets and not to philosophers.

That said, lots of things permeate everything I do and say and write. I know a thing or two about history (who can forget the infamous Pirenne Thesis? Or the geographic fetish of the Annales School?), I more than dabble in Weberian sociology, I know the difference between Freud and Jung, and I have about as much use for Skinner and his behaviorist claptrap as I do for the clap. Nowadays, they call that inter-disciplinarity, but I just call that being well read and having an active, living interest in the stuff of the world. We all live on the same planet, don't we? So why should we live in our individual ivory towers within a mega ivory tower?

At this point, you're probably thinking: Is there a point to all this or is there no point? The answer, naturally, is that there is. Of course there is: there always is, even if it's not immediately visible to those with impatient temperaments, superficial minds, and inferior educations. The question, as every writer knows, is: where to begin? At the beginning! is the obvious answer that occurs to the dull-witted. Those of us with sharper mental instruments know that the beginning is never the beginning and that the end is never the end. And yet, begin somewhere one must, because if one doesn't begin somewhere, nothing will get done or said. Note how cleverly we've come full circle. Having started my narrative with one counterfactual, I complete it with another counterfactual, sagely building uncertainty, contradiction, and paradox upon uncertainty, contradiction, and paradox. Will the result be a tower or a palimpsest? At Ardor Haus, I learned the answer could be neither or both.

***

The invitation arrived in late April or early May. I forget when exactly, although I do distinctly recall that the semester was mercifully nearing its end, that fragile student minds were migrating to a variety of destinations outside the assigned readings, and that I was counting the shamefaced tulips, roses, marigolds, and black-eyed Susans as they emerged, like bashful groundhogs, red and white and yellow and brown and blue, in the quadrangle, or Quad as we unimaginatively call it, in the geometric center of the college. Clouds were retreating like (get this) the Germans at Normandy Beach (powerful, no?), the sun had rediscovered its heavenly presence, and the hungry sparrows reappeared on the great lawns that, like mighty seas, sustain the towers, moats, ramparts, and castles of our tiny campus. I call it tiny, because, yes, it's darned tiny, consisting of several thousand truth-seeking students and several hundred truth-delivering faculty and Lord knows how many truth-evading administrators, secretaries, assistants, deans, vice deans, and vice-vice deans, all of whom multiply like poisonous mushrooms after a rainfall.

We're like Estonia or Singapore or Hong Kong or Israel, in that our size is our strength. But not our greatest strength. That's our diversity (if you're cringing upon having read the word, shame on you). I like to say our student body resembles the flowers in our Quad. Each individual stem-and-petal arrangement is gorgeous, a work of art, but put them all together and you've got an ensemble that surpasses any one flower in beauty and resembles a painting by Monet. His brushstrokes are sensitive, variegated, and sensuous, but it's their agglomeration on the quivering surface of a linen canvas that makes for a masterpiece. I'm proud to say our campus has been selected the most diverse tiny non-urban college for twenty-five years in a row by a leading Latin American survey of global higher education. That said, I'd be less than honest if I didn't suspect that our esteemed administration wasn't somehow manipulating the size, color, and shape of the student body to retain this distinction. One of my brighter female students (an Apache harpsichordist on a four-year scholarship from Truth or Consequence, New Mexico) once told me the college was practicing rampant sizism, colorism, and shapism, and I'm inclined to agree—not because I know anything about these things, but because she's one honest Native American Injun.

It's a rather civilized place, our campus. It was established back in the mid-nineteenth century thanks to a sizable grant by one of the region's more respectable robber barons. The fellow, reputedly a half-Irish, half-Russian immigrant who made his way across the ocean hidden under a greasy tarpaulin in the engine room of a banana boat, made his money scavenging garbage dumps for empty whiskey bottles and steak bones, grinding them into a fine powder, and mixing it with a variety of unnamable organic substances to produce low-grade fancy bricks. I can't vouch for their strength and durability, but the nouveau-riche farming class that made its money on corn liquor and pork bellies went gaga over the tiny bits of glitter and bought up the stuff like hotcakes. The president's house, which is just off campus in a lovely pine grove and lies next to a manmade pond that attracts all manner of annoyingly loud geese in the fall, used to be the Founder's villa (N.B. that he did not use his own bricks), where he lived with three or four wives, raised some ten children (whose framed oval portraits line the staircase in our library, reputed to be the very best among the category of colleges termed non-urban tiny), and caroused and drank and raised hell until a stroke finally laid him low on his ninety-third birthday. Rumor has it that his ghost still roams the halls of the villa, knocking over vases, tilting paintings, and stealing cigars from the president's *ther*midor (that is a pun and a backhanded comment on our beloved leader's IQ, so please laugh).

Portraits of the Founder—pardon the capital F, but it comes from force of habit, which, as we poets know, can be a liberator and a tyrant—adorn many of the buildings, including some common areas such as the faculty lounge, the men's rooms, and the student center. That wouldn't necessarily be a bad thing, and I sure as hell don't mind eating beneath our Founder's august gaze, but it's not just me who thinks the half-breed was exceptionally ugly: with a face like a melon, eyes like olives, a nose like a snail, and a mouth like worms (all items that, not incidentally, may on occasion be encountered in the food served in our lounge). In a word, he—or his portrait—personifies both opulence and decay. Everyone agrees he's no Adonis, but no one's ever said anything about his looks lest they (or he or she, if you prefer that form) be accused of lookism.

I still remember with a bit of dread the infamous luncheon several of us had with the dean, a thin biochemist with a face like a tennis racket who had somehow been persuaded that he understood the workings of an educational institution and was therefore qualified for the job. It was Hieronymus Chang, I think, who was perorating about something or other when he caught the Founder's jowly gaze and stopped in mid-word—not in mid-sentence, mind you, but in mid-word, something I've rarely if ever seen, and to top it all off it was a one-syllable word. Everyone's eyes turned to our robber baron's big, fat mug, but the dean cleared his throat, so loudly and so insistently that it was obvious to us all that he disapproved and that we had better get to the business of imbibing our wine (a passable Pinot Noir, I think) and munching on our Welsh rarebit. We did, of course, and Chang pursued his strand of thought almost without missing a beat, except of course that he did—miss a beat, I mean—and everyone knew he did and everyone knew there'd be a hefty price to pay. None of us was surprised to learn that Professor Hieronymus Chang decided to take early retirement next semester and that the Mathematics Department was explicitly forbidden to hire another unruly specialist in something as transgressive of good taste as Fibonacci numbers.

I should say a word or two about our president and dean. The president is a lady, and by that I don't just mean she's a woman, although she obviously is. She has skin like chipped porcelain, cheeks like overripe pairs, and hair like gray cotton candy. Born and raised in an English coal-mining town somewhere north of Newcastle, she got a free ride to Cambridge, "read," as the Brits say, anthropology or anthroposophy or some such thing, eventually defended a dissertation on the mating rituals of Birmingham's Hottentot minority, moved on to a directorship of one of the UK's most prominent talk shops and think tanks, and then, after weighing job offers from us and the International Monetary Fund, chose us. That was some ten years ago and she's been a smash with the students, faculty, and alumni since, having introduced, immediately upon arrival in our hallowed groves, Open House Fridays, during which we're all expected to sip sherry, munch on cucumber sandwiches and scones, and speak admiringly of the college. We do, of course—in any case, I do, which is why I've come to know the inside of the building as well as I do. By the way, the bathroom faucets are gold plated and the toilet paper is exceptionally soft.

Our dean, as I've already said, is a withered, wizened biochemist who thinks that colleges are organic compounds, that professors and students are molecules, and that education is best compared to Brownian motion. You can appreciate that even those professors and students who most resemble undifferentiated lumps of wet clay take some umbrage at what they see as his unjustified and unjustifiable chutzpah. Just about everyone hates the little man and his effectiveness as a leader has pretty much shrunk to nil. He says things, we pretend to listen; he does things, we pretend to be impressed; he issues commands, we pretend to carry them out. On the whole, it's a pleasant arrangement. Everyone feels empowered and, should it ever happen that you've had it up to here with the dean's moronic pronouncements, suddenly it's Friday and that means Open House and sherry, cucumber sandwiches, and scones at the president's villa. Life could be worse under the reign of Kristopher Robert Döner—known affectionately to his supporters as Kay-Bob and less affectionately to his critics as Döner Kabob. I doubt that most of our students get the reference, but our Balkan and Turkish exchange students think it's hilarious. As I always say: Thank God for diversity. (Note the upper-case G and the absence of an exclamation point: neither believers nor unbelievers need take offense.)

There's also the ever-present consolation of the sublime beauty of our campus and its environs. We have some ten or so redbrick buildings (why or so? Because two structures are glorified sheds that, not incidentally perhaps, house our poetry department and globalization program) with slender Ionic marble columns and Elizabethan thatched roofs (sic!), all designed by one of this country's most innovative nineteenth-century architects, Edmund Aristophanes Fygg, a Harvard-trained Boston Brahmin who gave up a promising career in the clergy for the noble pursuit of practical aesthetics, theoretical eugenics, and trans-historical memory. The thatched roofs (the straw, truth to tell, though it looks deceptively real, was converted to plastic sometime during the Roaring Twenties) usually strike most visitors to the campus as bold, perhaps a bit too bold—and I can certainly understand why the juxtaposition of plastic with Ferrara marble might elicit that kind of primary visceral reaction—but, after some thought and contemplation, they quickly come to appreciate the genius behind Fygg's invocation of ancient spirits from opposite temporal and spatial ends of the civilizational spectrum that is the culture of the Occident. Back in the nineteenth century, some Irish anarchists would protest whatever they happened to be protesting by setting fire to the roofs, but the president—it was, I believe, our third—settled the matter by banning matches on campus. We can proudly state that we've been smoke-free for over a century, well before the rest of the country saw the light on that one.

We're set in the middle of an invigorating pine forest, amid the inevitable rolling hills and rich farmland. Campuses usually are. The cliché insists that this be so and we dutifully bow our heads like vassals. Is that because land is cheapest amid rolling hills and rich farmland? Or is it because college founders seem to believe that rolling hills and rich farmland will be especially conducive to learning? Or is it just coincidence? Take your pick. I'd like to believe that aesthetically pleasing settings just naturally go together with the acquisition of deep knowledge and that campuses are as likely to produce rolling hills and rich farmland as rolling hills and rich farmland are likely to produce campuses. The world is a dialectical place, after all: it's damned big and awfully complex and only an appreciation of the backwards and forwards influences of both causes and effects can help us comprehend it deeply and fully, from the inside and the outside. (A friend of mine studies complexity and he's isolated no fewer than 461,382 factors that define our world. When I asked him how he knew the number was 461,382 and not 461,381 or 461,383, he just smiled elliptically.) I have no doubt that all things, however big or small and however concrete or abstract, have an inside and an outside. Not just a physical inside and outside—that would be a pretty banal observation—but an ontological and epistemological one too. Which is appearance and which is reality, however? Or are both equally real or equally unreal? Need I say that my views of reality were confirmed in glowing Technicolor at Ardor Haus?

Once or twice a week, regardless of weather, I go jogging in the forest and over the hills. At first, there's the sharp smell of the pines: it slaps your cheeks and intoxicates your mind and the only thing that your senses can consciously apprehend is the gentle crunching of the pine needles under foot. And then, just as the intoxication threatens to send you into a swoon (not unlike that experienced by a poet friend of mine who, she insists, truly swooned upon catching a glimpse of Ringo during the Beatles' first tour of the United States), the forest ends and before you rise luscious hills that quiver in the sunlight (erotically?) and abound with painterly effects whose sudden appearance actually pains, surprises, and delights me every time I see them. It's like running into a landscape by Seurat or Monet after inhaling the cold mountain air of a Homer (Winslow, that is: the other Homer, the Greek poet, did not, to my knowledge, paint). Beyond the hills are the neatly trimmed farms run by the bearded adherents of some religious sect. They speak an old dialect of French and, remaining true to the rigor of their founder, abjure all modern conveniences except for computers and mobile phones. Their women, by the way, wear no underpants. Don't ask me how I know.

We have a small lake and a stream—the words gurgling brook are actually quite apposite here, though I've purposely eschewed them, to avoid creating the impression that we happily wallow in kitsch. Their presence on campus is both good and bad. Good, because they're right there, never more than a few yards from any of the buildings. Bad, because, when the weather turns warm and the physicists, chemists, biologists, and other natural scientists trade their clothes for ill-shaped swimwear and dive into the placid lilied waters, the sight of so much pale cellulite quivering like fresh flan is almost enough to drive one to rhyme. It's odd, but I've noticed that scientists are usually as misshapen as they are shameless, while poets and writers are as shameful as they are dissolutely slim. So we leave the lake to the carousers who count atoms and murder mice and eye their antics with no small measure of tennis envy. But we get our revenge during Open House Fridays, when we, the humanists and social scientists, attack the sherry and cucumber sandwiches with a gusto and vigor that would elicit the unrestrained admiration of Genghis Khan and his fellow barbarians.

What else is there to say about the place? Ah, yes, one more thing. We have an especially distinguished faculty. More of our professors have been nominated for the Nobel Prize than on any other diverse tiny non-urban campus. And more of our faculty have been runners-up for Ford Foundation fellowships than any comparable faculty on any campus in the country. Our dean likes to say that, although we may not be the best in any one category, we're tenth best in every category—and that's better than best. Proof of the pudding is, I suppose, our exceptionally high EDI score, which measures the ratio of the ratio of excellence to diversity to the ratio of diversity to excellence. Our EDI was 0.85446, while Harvard's was a mere 0.64528. My statistician friends tell me that's very good.

***

As I was saying, the invitation arrived in late April or early

May in a thickish airmail envelope that had been posted in Italy. The stamp depicted a green profile of a desiccated man with a long nose. The return address said: Ardor Haus, Caravaggio-Milano. I confess to never having heard of the place and my first thought was to trash the envelope. Ardor Haus sounded like some kind of do-gooder NGO that was soliciting funds for its next do-gooder project in some exceptionally benighted part of the tenth world. (I am making a point: we are not tenth best, just as there is no tenth world.) What stopped me from dropping the letter in the plastic receptacle marked PAPER was the German spelling of house. What would a German NGO be doing in Italy's northern lake region? Was it a hangover from some South Tyrolean autonomist organization? Was it the pet project of a wealthy Nazi collaborator who managed to escape Bonn's bashful pursuit of post-war justice? Or was it, as the word ardor suggested, the handiwork of existentially confused sixty-eighters who, having abandoned Baader, Meinhof, and the socialist revolution, had discovered the unalloyed joys of flower power, pot, and the arts? That last possibility appealed to me. Who knew? Maybe they were looking for a poet to join their collective? I'd say no, of course, but it would be nice to know that my *oeuvre* had crossed the big pond and made it to *bella Italia*. And then I shivered (literally) as I realized that something as seemingly trivial as the spelling of two words consisting of three syllables and nine letters had stopped me from foregoing a possibly grand adventure. One could lose kingdoms for want of a nail, but, evidently, one could also win kingdoms *with* a nail!

I slit open the envelope, blew inside, thought for a moment that, blown up, it resembled an albino fish, and deftly removed a single sheet of paper and a glossy brochure. The letter was typewritten (on an old German-made Kolibri! O, shades of my youth!) and addressed to "The Honorable C. Milosz, Professor." That salutation was a nice touch, one that I had never before encountered in a letter, and it set me in the right frame of mind, which, obviously, was its intended purpose. The C, by the way, stands for Chester. I have some east Slavic blood—though I'm not sure whether it's Polish, Ukrainian, Rusyn, or something else or a mixture of Polish, Ukrainian, Rusyn, and something else—but we've always pronounced the family name as Millis. One of my girlfriends—a thin, chain-smoking Canadian woman with a long nose (why have so many long noses crossed my path in life?)—once wondered why I didn't just change it to Millis, but that just went to show how little she understood me and my work. (What can I say? She also had an inexplicable passion for Canadian cheese, which, I never failed to remind her, was really American cheese.) Poets may invent words (I once invented the word hove, as an amalgam of hate and love, but it did not catch on), but we always respect culture. After all, if it weren't for culture, where would we be? Our relationship didn't outlast that ill-fated remark, by the way.

"It gives us a great pleasure," the letter began, "to invite you to the global summit of the world's best minds." Well, I thought, your knowledge of English is a bit deficient, Señor Kolibri: it may give you great pleasure, but it should be a great honor. The indefinite and definite articles were annoying, but no matter: the letter writer could be forgiven for being a foreigner. Besides, the bit about best minds was a nice touch. Who was I to disagree? "We are convening the [sic!] five-day forum of leading global intellectuals, artists, businessmen [sic!], and policymakers to develop a multidimensional global blueprint for the world's future development as a harmonious globe." Oh, dear, I thought: three globals, two worlds, and one globe in just two sentences. It was clear that the Ardor Haus folks were aiming high. Perhaps too high? "Your outstanding contributions to the realm of poetry [why realm?] make you our first choice to represent the art of global poetry at our meeting." Outstanding? I've always thought so, but I must admit that the word has appeared only fleetingly on the lips of my critics. "In addition to yourself, we are inviting the flowing [sic] leading lights of global thought: Louise Babylon, Ariadne Balletmeister, Alla Belomorkanalskaya, Serge Joupanencoff, Orestes Heldenplatz, Thor Kriegman, Jean-Pierre La Baguette, Dickey Lemon, Hal Lumumba, Sanjay "Svven" Palermo, Emilia de Pouff, Samuel Livingston Roach, Stefan von Troubadour, Bogusława Wielkomała, Alexandra Wirrwarr, and Joe Zsasz. These great minds obviously need no introductions."

Quite the contrary, I hadn't heard of any of these luminaries (except perhaps for Kriegman, whose name rang some distant bell from the world of journalism), but that didn't trouble me, as I was certain that none of them was a poet and I would've been distressed only if they were. It seemed like an interesting, diverse group, more or less evenly balanced between men and women, and obviously drawn from various parts of the world. There followed a few lines about what we'd be doing—"dialoguing and interrogating global problems and prospects"—and what we were expected to produce—"the ten commandments for a new world"—and then they assured me that all my travel expenses ("first class in an airline of your choice") would be covered and that they'd be honored—that part was redundant in light of the first line—if I accepted, and so on and so forth. The letter was signed by three people: "Joe Zsasz, summit organizer; Dickey Lemon, funder; Malvina Florentina, Ardor Haus director." Zsasz's name, I noticed, was a palindrome. How did he pronounce it? As Zaz? As Sass? Or as Zass? I had no idea. My interest piqued, I knew that, if only for this reason, I'd have to accept the invitation.

There was another reason, one that shamed me. I had been suffering from writer's block (not to be confused with writer's block, which is one's lifelong creative *oeuvre*) for several years, for so long, in fact, that I had stopped counting. I was certain it'd melt away one day, but I was worried that, the longer it took, the slimmer my chances of winning the Nobel Prize would be. I know what you're thinking: Chester Milosz, forget it. You'll never get to go to Oslo. Probably, but, as they say, nothing attempted with enthusiasm, nothing attained. You may call that cheek, but I call it a realistic calculation of the odds. Were my chances of grabbing a Nobel great? Of course not. But would they get decidedly worse if the block of ice remained in place? Of course. Perhaps Ardor Haus would joggle my creative innards and get me going again. Or perhaps not. Either way, there was only one way to find out. *On s'engage et puis on voit*, as Napoleon said—not, I hoped, before the Battle of Waterloo

I'm not sure how it happened, but I do distinctly remember putting the finishing touches on a poem in early December, just as the fall semester was coming to an end, and feeling quite pleased with the subtle way I had managed to give both Eros and Thanatos their due without detracting from the leitmotif—the human condition, of course. I then boarded a plane for Jamaica, where I had been invited to attend a poetry festival organized by the Montego Bay Coffee Growers Association. Four days in the sun seemed like just the thing I needed in preparation for the harsh winter months, but the stiflingly hot and humid air depressed me and a quick swim in the ocean resulted in a bad sunburn that drained me of whatever residual enthusiasm I had for the gathering. I read poorly, desultorily, mechanically, and the audience knew it and responded accordingly. As did a few of the more temperamental coffee-growers with decidedly anti-Yanqui inclinations. I got drunk on rum on the flight back and, after dropping my bags on the kitchen table and knocking over a vase, fell into bed, slept some twenty hours, and awoke with a terrible hangover. I haven't felt like writing since. I'm not even sure it's writer's block; it's more like writer's lack of interest, which arguably is a far worse thing. I figured a jaunt to the land that gave birth to Vergil, Dante, and D'Annunzio could only do me some good. Five days of hobnobbing with global minds might just liberate my unfortunate Muses (bound like those dullards in Plato's cave) and set them flying again, though not, I trusted, like Icarus. Northern Italy was also wine country and a brief romp in the vineyards with Bacchus couldn't possibly hurt. The summit was scheduled for mid-summer, so there was nothing to stop me from going. And besides, the jogging would surely be no worse there than here. I would have to pack my sneakers.

I was also intrigued by Ardor Haus. As I read the brochure, I realized that the story behind the place outdid my wildest speculations. It turned out that Ardor Haus was the offspring of the Otto Nabokov Foundation, which in turn was the brainchild of the billionaire industrialist and philanthropist, Otto Nabokov. That wasn't terribly interesting, but Otto's personal background was. He was, apparently, some distant cousin of Vladimir, the great Russian-American writer and a fellow professor at, if I'm not mistaken, Finger Lake Community College (a sad place, by the way: how Vlad managed to survive and thrive there is quite beyond me). After the Nabokovs fled the Bolshies and settled in Berlin—where Vladimir's politically engaged *papasha* took a bullet from a crazed Russian monarchist—Vladimir's father's brother's third cousin, a dissolute young man by the name of Nikolai Efimovich Nabokov, married the homely daughter of a rich Prussian Junker named von und zu Berlowitz and, after his father-in-law's unfortunate demise during the street fighting of the mid-twenties—he was struck through the heart by a drunken Freikorps nationalist's *Pickelhaube* and died on the spot—inherited a small fortune. Otto's mother died in childbirth and, as Nikolai's only son, Otto became a very rich man upon his father's death, also, ironically, at the hands of a crazed Russian monarchist. (Why so many crazed Russian monarchists were on the loose and why they all displayed a disturbing proclivity to employ firearms in settling real or imagined disputes I honestly did not know.)

Later in life, Otto came upon Vladimir's masterpiece, *Ada*, at an airport souvenir shop—it was stuck between a lavish edition of Tristan Tzara's Dada poems and a popular biography of Idi Amin Dada—and, becoming enamored of the book and its author, did a bit of research and was both pleased and shocked to learn that the late lepidopterist was a blood relative. It was then, apparently, that Otto decided to honor Uncle Vlad's memory by establishing a foundation and a quiet place for great minds to meet and contemplate the world. He had originally wanted to call the retreat Ada House, until one of his well-paid advisors reminded him that that was the moniker of an American stripper-singer who had scandalized Europe with her salacious kiwi act. What to do? The ever-resilient and quick-footed Otto noticed that the full title of the novel was actually *Ada or Ardor: A Family Chronicle*. Well, that settled that and Ardor Haus was born. No one could confuse its name with the stripper's: so much was clear. The childless Otto had passed away some years ago—in bed, thereby breaking the chain of bullet-induced demises that had plagued the family—but the foundation and the retreat were well taken care of in his last testament and, under the resourceful leadership of Malvina Florentina, the former chief executive officer of a major Italian multinational that traded in all manner of natural resources, had established themselves as leaders in the world of deep-pocketed philanthropy and even deeper thought.

I liked Otto. He seemed like a modest guy who was looking for his roots and decided to do some good in the process. Their being Slavic roots helped. The Miloszes were hardly as distinguished as the Nabokovs—I knew for a fact that none of my ancestors had ever been assassinated by monarchists or republicans, crazed or not—but they came from the same part of the world as Otto's people and probably followed a similar path to get to this country. That was something. True, my folks hadn't a drop of blue blood in them, at least as far as I knew; they had been peasants or peasants-turned-workers who fled, not revolution, but the school-of-hard-knocks immiseration that ole Karl predicted would lead to revolution. They tilled the soil in the tiny village of Przebrzegorzwice, located in one of the many verdant valleys that dot the overlapping foothills of the Tatra, Beskid, and Carpathian mountains.

Przebrzegorzwice was no paradise. Illiteracy was near-universal, hygiene was unknown, and syphilis was rampant, but the hard-working folk were happy with the little they had, until the day the Austro-Hungarians extended a dirt road from the neighboring valley and the Przebrzegorzwicens came to realize that, were it not for the cartographical efforts of an Enlightenment-besotted Magyar nobleman who took a wrong turn in the forest and stumbled upon their village, they had until then not even existed in the mind's eye of the authorities. Discovery proved to be a disaster. True, Przebrzegorzwice got a school, a sewer, and a gendarme, but it also got taxes, with the result that centuries of living anarchically outside the bounds of the law led many natives to wrap their meager possessions in bundles and alight the dirt road to the neighboring valley. Within a generation, the entire population had emigrated, including all the Miloszes. Decades of decay followed. That turned out to be a blessing, as no one cared to occupy or pillage the village in the two big wars of the twentieth-century world. Eventually, German tourism sparked by the *Wirtschaftswunder* saved the day. The village has now become a spa and the former school has been enlarged and renovated and now houses a four-star hotel known for its slow-food cuisine and commitment to locally grown farm produce. Even the caviar comes from a salt-water fish farm located just behind the hotel and designed by an Azeri-German engineering concern that hopes to attract American tourists by changing the town's name to Zebraville and introducing something called the Zebraburger.

It was sometime before or after the first Great War that Granddad Milosz worked his way across the ocean on the Édouard Herriot, a turn-of-the century French steamer laden with rotting Ukrainian wheat. I assume he still pronounced the family name Mee-Losh; it may have been his encounter with the linguistic obtuseness of the local authorities on Elvis Island that convinced him to consider changing the pronunciation. Granddad eventually found lodging somewhere on the Lower East Side, at the very top of a six-floor tenement with no running water and no toilet. That circumstance—and the fact of a small bladder, something I appear to have inherited from my grandfather—appears to have cured him of his predilection for ample amounts of alcohol, a habit he picked up, along with everybody else, in Przebrzegorzwice. That turned out to be another blessing (how many have there been thus far—two?), not just because it saved his liver from irreversible decay, but also because it led to his joining a fanatical temperance group, working his way up to the rank of captain (which entailed acquiring a navy-blue jacket with golden shoulder braids), and eventually finding secure employment—and a wife. It just so happened that my grandmother hailed from the neighboring valley with the dirt road that proved to be the source of Przebrzegorzwice's downfall. Granddad might not have been able to forgive her that, were it not for her descent into a perpetual state of drunkenness in the tough sailor bars on Cherry Street, which his anti-temperance group had targeted for a high-priority clean-up. He found her lying in last night's sawdust; she looked up at what she initially thought was a policeman, their eyes met, and both knew, as they later claimed, that they had encountered their destiny. A week later, she took a bath and they got married.

My father was born nine months later, almost to the day. They named him Emiliano, a bizarre name for a proud descendent of Przebrzegorzwice, but one that made perfect sense in the Italian neighborhood where my grandparents had a basement apartment that lacked light, was perpetually cold and damp, and was infested with rats, but had the inestimable advantage of being a few steps from the outhouse in the backyard. I once found a dog-eared dime novel on one of Granddad's shelves: *Bandidos! The Thrilling Story of Pancho Villa and Emiliano Zapata*. Every second word was underlined, awkward translations were scribbled in the margins, and I could see from the greasy pages that he had used it to study English. That certainly explained his unusual locutions—two of his favorites were to call me a *bandido* and to tell his nagging wife that he'd do chores *mañana*—but it also revealed the likely origins of my Slavic father's unusual name. Did Granddad think Italians spoke Spanish? Or that Italian was Spanish? Could be. Inebriated south Europeans probably looked all the same to him.

Granddad definitely didn't expect his choice of name to influence my father's life as much as it did. Dad was short and swarthy and, with a name like Emiliano, could easily pass for a Sicilian. By the time he turned eight, he was running errands for the local organized-crime don. At sixteen, he dropped out of high school and sold "insurance" (Granddad: "heh-heh") to local storekeepers. By twenty, the don promoted him to the ranks of his enforcers. Granddad and Grandma were distraught that their flesh and blood had turned into a rotten apple. They threatened to disown him, but my father just laughed (Granddad: "ha, ha, ha"). They threatened to denounce him to the police, but he knew they were bluffing. Emiliano seemed to be on the fast track to hell until, one day, the inevitable happened: he met a nice girl, my future mother, who convinced him to go straight. He did, but not before ratting on the don's crime family to the cops. He got off easy and, after two years in the singsong setting of Sing, where he consumed all the torts in the prison library (to tell the truth, I always thought he was just sublimating his boundless appetite for sweets) and completed a distance-learning degree in law, he emerged from the bowels of incarceration a newly-minted lawyer committed to fighting crime.

Nine months later, almost to the day, I entered the world. Why my parents named me Chester I don't know, but it may have had something to do with Pop's genuine admiration for President Chester Arthur, a man he always insisted was terribly underrated by historians and the legal profession. Unfortunately, Emiliano Milosz's career as a crime fighter never took off—probably because his white-shoe colleagues at the bar held a low regard for his unsavory past—and Pop spent the rest of his life filling out tax returns and searching for tax loopholes—which he did assiduously, as, perhaps, a form of revenge for being excluded from the upper echelons of the profession. Our family never paid any taxes, not by cheating, mind you, but by funneling whatever spare cash we had into real estate holdings in down-and-out neighborhoods along the riverfront. That turned out to be a brilliant move. As the police drove out the prostitutes, closed down the S&M bars, and cracked down on narcotics trafficking, well-heeled investment bankers bought up the brownstones and townhouses and the slums Pop owned turned into gold mines. But not for long. When the authorities resolved to build a highway along the waterfront, they bought us out for a fraction of the market value and Pop took the gun the don gave him in an earlier life and blew out his brains, leaving behind a note of protest. Next day's headline in the yellow press—"Ex-Con Tax Lawyer to City: Bang-Bang, I'm Dead"—so unnerved my mother (as much by its crudeness as by its mendacious implication that Pop shot himself twice, something that Mom knew was antithetical to the penny-pinching habits of her late husband) that she went into a deep depression and, several weeks later, passed away in her sleep.

I had just begun working on my dissertation—it was going to be a comparative Lacanian deconstruction of Homer's *Iliad* and Vergil's *Aeneid*—and, having inherited my parents' money, I became the darling of the coeds and my department overnight. But why analyze poetry when I now had the wherewithal to write it? I self-published my first collection, *Last Things First*, a year later. Although it got no reviews, it did attract the interest of the editor of a small university press who offered me a contract for a second volume. That turned out to be *First Things Last*, which garnered me a Beulitzer and a slew of teaching offers. I accepted, they gave me tenure and a named chair, and lo, I became Professor Chester Milosz, poet extraordinaire. Which pretty much brings the story up to the present. And which may also explain why I'm confident about winning a Nobel—assuming I can overcome that writer's block, of course, and resume expanding my writer's block.

***

I first took an Air France flight to Paris, where I paid my respects to Piaf, Morrison, and the Communards at Père Lachaise and to Ionesco, Petliura, and Sontag at Montparnasse, tried to catch a glimpse of the Mona Lisa at the Louvre (but was frustrated in my efforts by a phalanx of video-wielding Japanese tourists), stopped at the Librairie polonaise on Saint Germain to see if they had translations of my books (they did, in distressingly large numbers, I'm afraid), had a late lunch (Coquilles Saint Jacques, escargots, and a bottle of Chateau Magritte) with a minor French poet who has never been able to forgive me my Beulitzer (and who, obnoxiously, pronounces it boo-leet-ZAY), meandered up to Place Pigalle, where I had a delicious Nutella crêpe, and caught the first show at the Crazy Horse (Moonie Trafalgar was in her usual excellent shape, especially in that cartwheel number). Next morning, Alitalia brought me safely to Milano, where I had booked a room in a small *albergo* a few blocks from Mussolini's imposing train station. The streets were lined with busty streetwalkers in skin-tight minis and coal-black Africans in striped dashikis selling faux-designer handbags, but the hotel actually catered to tourists, mostly Russians, as far as I could tell, and especially loud Russians at that. As I was turning the key in the lock to my door, three of them emerged, quite blotto, from the adjacent room. One embraced me, another handed me a bottle of vodka, and the third proceeded to unzip his fly and urinate in the hallway. It turned out they were all members of the Russian Duma and were in Milano on some democracy-promotion exercise funded by the European Union. Igor, Stanislav, and Vladimir were their names, and we quickly became good friends. Or so I think.

They checked out next day and, after I awoke, I confess to having no recollection of the preceding day. My wallet and passport hadn't been touched, but a copy of *First Things Last* (I had brought five, just in case) had been pilfered. How could I be angry? Art trumped life once again and, better still, Chester Milosz had finally penetrated the Russian market! Unlike some friends of mine who were Mother Russia lovers, I have always viewed the place as a cross between the worst of Europe and the best of Asia and have never concealed my skepticism. How would the Russkies respond to my withering condemnation of dictatorship, "Akh, akh, Akhmatova!"? Western critics called it a masterpiece—and one German (the drama critic for the *Regensburger Handelsblatt*) even termed it "*besser*" than Faust—but how would the core of Eurasia respond? As "*luchshe*" than Tolstoy or just a pale copy of late Yevtushenko? I'd find out soon enough, after Igor, Stanislav, or Vladimir put my book in circulation and a pirated translation appeared in some provincial press.

A double espresso *corretto* Sambuca reestablished my bearings, while the orange trolleys sailing along the shadows of the tree-lined boulevards reminded me that imagery was my domain and that poetry was my métier. I felt inspired to write a sonnet—had the writer's block dissolved along with the vodka in my bloodstream?—and decided that the roof of the Duomo would be the perfect setting for such a momentous event. Thence I could observe Vergil's fair offspring amid the ochre- and slate-colored rooftops of the city. A gentle breeze would caress my lips and the persistent cooing of doves would remind me of the mortality of man. As with so much in life, however, I had made a slight miscalculation with momentous consequences. I had no local currency and, after being turned back at the turnstile by a little uniformed Italian with a twisted moustache and an oily voice, I was compelled by *force majeure* to find a bank, stand in line, and express annoyance at the preposterous exchange rate and service fee. By the time I stepped into the glorious sunlight of the Piazza Duomo, my Muses had abandoned me once again. To hell with them, I thought, as I downed a grappa and attended to its slow, warm descent into my gut. Still, their reappearance, however temporary, was a good sign. Surely, having just graced me with their heavenly presence, they would come again.

As I surveyed the lunch menu at the Ristorante Mediterraneo, I resolved to name my next collection *Last Things Last*. It went without saying that the fourth book would have the, at first glance, obvious title, *First Things First*, but I hoped that my critics and readers would appreciate the irony of its appearing last (as a self-reflexive act of auto-deconstruction!). But there was time to fret about these details later. Meanwhile, getting rid of this damned writer's block was the order of the day. I knew I couldn't just will it away. Indeed, the sad experience of the last few years had amply demonstrated that the more I applied myself, the more intractable it became. It was like a stubborn mule. If it refused to budge, no amount of whacking or pleading could make it move. The encouraging news was that mules eventually did move, presumably because they were hungry or thirsty or began to feel uncomfortable standing in their own excrement in the hot sun.

I took a sip of the Chianti as the waitress slipped the pizza margherita onto my table, curtsied, and disappeared. My gaze focused on a Lollobrigida-like brunette with a poodle in one arm and a balding man on the other. She stopped in mid-stride, dropped the dog, and slapped her companion. He slapped her back, picked up the confused animal, took her by the arm, and they resumed walking. Had I just witnessed a quarrel or a ritual? What impressed me most was the casual indifference both parties had exhibited. This unexpected insight, I suddenly realized, made the mule of my writer's block move, if only an inch. The lesson was obvious. I would have to cultivate that same indifference toward my Muses. Let them stand in their own excrement in the hot sun: I would not care. Naturally, the indifference would have to be real, not feigned. I drained the glass and motioned to the waitress for another Chianti. On the other hand, so what if the indifference were feigned and not real? Why should the Muses notice? Where did it say that inspirers of creativity had to be good observers of human behavior?

Fair enough, but how was I to *not* think about *not* writing? (To not write about not thinking seemed immeasurably easier, though I'm not sure why.) How could two non-grammatical negatives amid split infinitives produce a dispositional positive? How could two absences result in a presence? The philosophical or, perhaps, theological sophistication that answering these questions required was beyond my modest capabilities. Reading Wittgenstein didn't mean one was Wittgenstein and misreading Heidegger sure as hell didn't mean one was Heidegger. Who was I? Chester Milosz. What was I? A poet and a human being. What did human beings do? Live. What did poets do? Write. But I knew that—I knew it all too well—and it was obvious that this line of thought only led to a vicious circle. I looked up from my pizza and saw Lollobrigida and her man approaching. They had, evidently, been out for a stroll and were retracing their steps. Once again, they paused in front of the restaurant: this time, the poodle was on a leash, prancing about gaily, while she stroked his cheek and he stroked hers.

Suddenly, I felt I was breaking free of the vicious circle (but not yet, I can state with hindsight, of the parentheses) that had imprisoned me: here was poetry in action. All I had to do was breathe and I would find it all around me. No, that formulation wasn't quite right: *it* (poetry) would find *me* (Chester Milosz, poet). The booleet-ZAY—a wisp of a smile adorned my lips as I thought of my mediocre French poet-*ami*—was only the first of many laurels that would crown my head like Caesar's. How appropriate that I should be in the cradle of Roman civilization. How right it was for me to be having these thoughts on the Piazza Duomo. The Chianti and pizza were the bread and wine of my conversion. And Ardor Haus would, I felt certain, serve as my springboard to Oslo and the Nobel.

***

The black limousine was waiting in front of my *albergo* as I stepped onto the sidewalk and breathed in the cool morning air. The painted whores were gone and the bony Africans had only just begun unrolling their blankets and removing the Guccis from large plastic garbage sacks. An orange trolley rattled past along the avenue to my right. Three black-clad nuns with long rosaries swinging from their necks hurried past. A large beige dog lay asleep in front of the Tabacchi. A short uniformed driver emerged from the sleek vehicle and motioned to my well-traveled suitcases.

"Alberto." His smile was both viscous and pencil thin. "*Buon giorno*. Eh, you—Ardora Howze?"

"*Si*, Ardora Howze." I smiled back and handed him the luggage.

"We go, *si*?"

"We go, *si*. But first, coffee. *Caffè*, OK?"

"OK, I also. *Caffè*. OK?"

"OK."

We stepped into the Bar Marinetti and took our places at the curved aluminum bar. The Italians, all resembling businessmen in a hurry, were munching on crème-filled croissants and sipping tiny espressos. Their excited chatter and the clatter of spoons stirring sugar, cups striking saucers, and coins clanging in the cash register momentarily confused me. It took me a second to reestablish my bearings and realize that Alberto was tugging at my sleeve.

"*Due caffès corretti* grappa, OK? You, me, *caffès*, OK?"

"No," I said with some alarm. "No *due*, no *due*. I don't think that would be quite appropriate so early in the morning and, besides, you're about to drive—"

"OK, OK, *capisco*," his eyes glistened, "no you, only me, *due*. You—later, OK?" His eyelids fluttered like butterflies as he lowered his voice. "You want woman, eh?"

"No," I stuttered. "No woman, *grazie*."

"Man? Boy? Nice. I know: *tutti*?"

"No, thank you," I said with greater confidence, "no man, no boy, no *tutti*," and, as the bartender placed two caffès *corretti* grappa on the counter, I grabbed one. Alberto poured an avalanche of sugar into his, stirred vigorously, and slurped the syrupy liquid. Then he grinned, revealing one gold tooth, and replaced the cup on the saucer, which, I noticed, was chipped.

"Maybe woman later, OK? Now"—and he placed his left hand on my elbow—"we go, eh? Time"—he tapped his watch—"late. How you say? *Tempus fugit*. OK?"

***

We sped along the highway as if the limo were a hotrod on Route 66, heading northwest. Motionless aircraft, seemingly suspended like toy planes from the puffy clouds that dotted the sky on our left, reflected the morning sun like shards of glass. Alberto drove silently, his gloved hands glued to the wheel and his gaze focused on some distant vanishing point. As we passed the traffic, I noticed we were doing one hundred sixty kilometers (which, when multiplied by 0.6, equaled ninety-six miles per hour!). Good heavens! is what I wanted to say. Instead:

"Very fast" is what I said. "Don't you think we should—?"

"*Si*," he nodded and promptly accelerated.

About an hour outside of Milano, as rows of grape vines stretched out to our right and purple-blue mountains shimmered nervously before us, the traffic slowed and then, after a hundred yards, fully stopped. Alberto put the car into neutral and placed a disc into the CD player. "Adriano Celentano. You like?" I lowered the tinted-glass window and stuck my head out. Just up ahead, red lights were flashing amid curling wisps of sooty smoke. An ambulance, its siren blaring, scurried along the shoulder. Alberto yawned and turned up the volume. "This song I love, *multo bene*." The arrangement was unusual, but I immediately recognized the melody and the lyrics: "One, two, three o' clock, four o' clock rock—Five, six, seven o' clock, eight o' clock rock—Nine, ten, eleven o' clock, twelve o' clock rock—We gonna rock around the clock tonight."

"That's Bill Haley and the Comets."

"No Beel Helee. Adriano Celentano."

"They're an American band."

"No *americano*: Celentano *italiano*."

"Yes, I know," I said, "but the song was first sung by Bill Haley and the Comets. As a matter of fact, it's considered to be the first rock n' roll song."

"Celentano *italiano*," Alberto sighed, "and"—this time with a combination of exasperation and finality—"song *italiano*."

I let the matter drop. The traffic began moving. Alberto shifted gears as if he were throttling a hen and we jerked forward. The police had cordoned off one lane. One officer directed oncoming vehicles with desultory motions of his right hand. Two white-clad paramedics were pushing a stretcher toward the back of an ambulance. Several others were crouching near the smoldering wreck of a red Fiat. A bitter smell permeated the air and I closed my window. Alberto was tapping the wheel as he turned gently to the left.

"Leessen," he faced me with a broad smile, "very good now."

Celentano did a rousing, if accented rendition of the refrain—"We're gonna rock around the clock tonight. We're gonna rock, rock, rock 'til broad daylight. We're gonna rock, we're gonna rock around the clock tonight"—but I said nothing. As we accelerated and I turned my head to catch a last glimpse of the flashing lights and white coats, I realized I had been tapping my foot.

"Yes, it's very good," I said.

"There"—Alberto pointed at the mountains—"Ardora Howze."

***

Just after we took the exit north, into the mountains, Alberto pulled into a narrow, poplar-lined lane that curved sharply to the right and culminated in a parking lot and a flat whitewashed building with a flashing neon sign announcing Bar-Ristorante Benito. He slipped the car between two shiny Mercedes, nodded approvingly, and grunted, "Russos." The air was spicy and warm and I inhaled deeply. This sure beat the campus, even with its pond-like lake, babbling stream (why shouldn't streams babble as much as brooks?), and deliciously green rolling hills. It took my eyes several seconds to adjust to the darkness of the place. A dusty chandelier with several dark bulbs adorned the center of the ceiling. A curved bar occupied one corner. The rest of the room was filled with small round tables with checkered tablecloths and flickering candles. Three of the tables in the far corner had been set together. Seated there were four large men, with golden bracelets and flashy necklaces and dressed in blue Adidas tracksuits.

"Russos," Alberto sniffed and shook his head sadly, as if in reluctant appreciation of their inferior cultural status. "Many—in Italia. *Tutti* Mafia."

"*Tutti*? Really?"

"*Si, tutti*." He wiped away what may have been a tear.

We sat in the corner diagonally opposite from the Russians who spoke in low tones and appeared to be conferring. Alberto motioned at them with his eyebrows, tapped the side of his hip, and said, "Bang-bang." I pretended to look for the waiter and espied what appeared to be longish lumps in their back pockets.

"Guns?"

"*Si, tutti* Mafia. *Due caffès corretti* grappa?"

"No!" I almost roared in response.

"OK, OK, *capisco*." Alberto waved to the bar tender. "*Per favore, signore, due caffès corretti* Sambuca."

One of the Russians turned his elephantine head in our direction and greeted us with a smirk. He tugged on his chain and turned back to the group. They were, I assumed, drinking vodka and probably regarded our preference for liqueurs cut with coffee as effeminate. Did they think we were a homosexual couple? The fey Italian and his Amerikanski master? I was still deep in thought (more like skin deep, to tell the truth), as the waitress brought us our coffees and two cold glasses of vodka. One moment later, the big Russian with the smirk pulled up a chair and deposited his oversized thighs into it with an extended wheeze. The table shuddered (literally) and the vodka quivered.

"Amereeken?" he asked. Alberto smiled confidently and nodded at me.

"Amereeken?" he repeated.

"Yes," I said. "I'm American."

"You kheff dollarz?"

"No," I shook my head, "I only carry plastic."

"Plah-steek?"

"Credit cards."

"Ah." He sounded disappointed, like a card player who'd just been dealt a lousy hand.

"No dollars, just credit cards. All Americans do. It's the only way to travel, you know, much more convenient than—." I stopped in mid-sentence after realizing I was chattering nervously. Better to project self-confidence, I thought. "Yes," I repeated slowly, "no dollars, just plastic."

"You my friend?" he asked, seemingly hurt. Frankly, the *non sequitur* shocked me and for a second I wondered whether he was aware of his well-timed philosophical *faux pas*.

"Why, yes, of course." I decided to nod wisely, but he looked disappointed, distressed, and dispirited. (My words, not his.)

"So plees why Amereeka no you-my-friend Rasha?" His eyes bore into mine. "Why Amereeka no you-my-friend Rasha? Huh? Why Amereeka boom-boom Rasha?" He appeared to pause for effect before skewering me with his final questions: "Why Amereeka you-my-friend Ukraina? Why Amereeka you-my-friend Polahnd?

Huh?"

Nonplussed (he reminded me of my students, so I felt fully in control), I coolly countered: "But, my friend, Amereeka you-my-friend Russia, Amereeka you-my-friend Ukraine, and Amereeka you-my-friend Poland. America no boom-boom Russia and America no boom-boom Ukraine and America no boom-boom Poland." I leaned back satisfied with my off-the cuff resolution of Eastern Europe's complex geopolitics. Henry Kissinger couldn't have done better. Talleyrand would have been proud. What could my Eurasian interlocutor say to my swift, elegant, and rapier-like riposte?

The big Russian sat silently for several seconds. Then his eyes brightened and, after shouting, "*Tovarishch!*" he seized one of the vodka glasses and downed its contents in one swift motion. As he rose from the table, he struck me on the back, placed a wet kiss on my forehead, and growled, "You OK, *tovarishch*." I smiled back weakly, while Alberto flashed his teeth and intoned, "*Si, si, americano* OK."

***

Once in the mountains, Alberto slowed down to some one hundred twenty kilometers, barely reducing speed while taking curves or gliding past towns and villages. We brushed against bushes several times and twice he had to blow his horn maniacally in order to avoid hitting stationary cyclists pedaling furiously up hills. At times, we dove (not a typo!) straight into the sun and, when it suddenly reappeared from behind the pine trees, the blinding glare created the momentary illusion of a flight through space that usually ended with Alberto's hasty application of the brakes and swift turn back into our lane. Finally, the car ascended a steep mountain, decelerating progressively in the process, and, when we reached the apex, before us extended a magnificent vista: a silver-coated lake that snaked its way amid snowcapped mountains dotted with orange villas. As we began our descent, Alberto pointed to the town below and said, "Caravaggio. Small ceety. Ardora Howze. Ten meenutes, maybe twenee."

Caravaggio—no relation, as I later learned, to the painter—was an upscale resort town with heavily perfumed air and a cobblestoned main street lined with expensive automobiles, flashy women, suntanned men, designer boutiques, and outdoor cafés. Crooked alleys ended in steep stone stairs on the right and glimpses of the shiny water on the left. A basilica with a huge pale-green rotunda, an imposing marble staircase, and rows of white columns dominated the main square. "Santa Maria Dolorosa," Alberto said as we bypassed the piazza and made a sharp right turn at a McDonald's. The tourists were a source of great annoyance to Alberto and he honked incessantly. A boy on a skateboard gave us the finger. An exceedingly pale man in a white three-piece suit and bowtie poked at the car with his umbrella but missed.

"*Turisti!*" Alberto slapped his forehead in exasperation. "But Caravaggio—nice, very nice, *si*?"

A few minutes later, we emerged from the labyrinth of *vias* and *viales* and pulled up before an ornate metal gate. "Ardora Howze!" Alberto beamed. "Nice, *si*?" He said something into a telephone, the massive gate creaked open, and we proceeded down a serpentine path toward the villa. Tall cypress trees swayed in the breeze like ostrich feathers. Set back from the road were marble statues of what I took to be gods and goddesses surrounded by blue, pink, and white hydrangea bushes. Off to the left was a lawn covered entirely with lavender. The buzzing and clicking of cicadas formed a backdrop to this cornucopia of colors and smells. Our wheels crackled as we slid to a stop on the gravely parking space before the villa, an ochre-colored Roman-style structure with rounded red clay roof shingles and slender columns on all its sides. A black mini-van stood in the lot and a group of some twenty people were milling about a pile of luggage, to which a dark-skinned boy with a gleaming wet forehead was adding pieces from the back of the vehicle.

Like a penguin, Alberto trundled over with my suitcases in his hands and deposited them near the others. I followed, surveying what were, evidently, the participants of the "global summit." So these were the "world's best minds." They didn't look like the world's best minds, but, then again, I had to admit I had no idea how the best minds—or, for that matter, even exceptionally good minds—looked. They looked like my colleagues back home and, as deep as my respect for them was (no irony intended, so please restrain that grin), I knew quite well that they fell a tad short of the best-mind category. This bunch was mostly attired in jeans and khakis; a few had jackets (one of which, I noticed, was linen); only three of the women wore skirts or dresses; and everybody's eyes were protected by sunglasses. But protected from what? The sun, to be sure, but also, I suspected, from the prying eyes of the other great minds. The pile grew larger and the dark-skinned boy was audibly grunting with every heave. I assumed they had been instructed to wait for all the luggage to be unloaded before they could take theirs and proceed to the registration desk. As the boy finally cried, "*Basta,*" I stepped forward, grabbed my suitcases, and froze. For there, resting atop the pile was a pair of soiled men's Ralph Lauren jockey shorts. Unable to resist a smile, I strategically positioned myself behind the pile and watched the Underwear Incident unfold.

Whose were the shorts and how would the great minds react upon seeing them? And, most important, would anyone claim them? A distinguished-looking, gray-haired gentleman caught my eye. He appeared to be unusually ill at ease, continually fidgeting with his upturned mustache. Was he the one? Or was it the stocky little man with huge eyes nervously puffing on a cigarette? I hadn't paid attention to the size of the shorts, but I knew that cigarettes often served to camouflage insecurities and create devil-may-care impressions. And how could I be certain that the owner wasn't a woman with peculiar predilections or understandable preferences for cotton underthings? The aging hippie over there might be just the one.

Fortunately, the group didn't rush the luggage all at once. The first to approach was a middle-aged woman with red lipstick. She removed her sunglasses and, upon seeing the shorts, raised her eyebrows, tugged at a handle, replaced her glasses, and moved on. Next came the distinguished-looking, gray-haired gentleman. He paused, with the shorts no more than twelve inches from his face, intently examined the pile, deliberately moving his head from left to right and from right to left, emitted a brief "Ah" (but the tone, unlike that of the big Russian in the Benito, was expectant), and, like a highly-paid Park Avenue surgeon, extracted his suitcase from the middle of the pile, careful not to disturb it and the shorts. The stocky little man was third. He kept the cigarette precariously balanced on his lower lip in Camus-like fashion and, while squinting (from embarrassment or from the acrid smoke?), seized two leather bags and, after sneezing vigorously, dropping the cigarette (which he then carefully stepped on with his tasseled brown shoe), and wiping his nose with a silken handkerchief, retreated to the villa. His was either a bravura performance or a sincere display of awkwardness. I knew then that the remaining fifteen or so people would negotiate the underwear with equal doses of real or feigned nonchalance.

When they had all departed for the villa, only Alberto, the shorts, and I remained. They had progressively lost in altitude with every piece of withdrawn luggage and, by the end, lay crumpled, like the flag of a defeated king, amid the dust and gravel. Their pose was both ludicrous and tragic, especially in such imperial surroundings. Was this a commentary on the frailty of human existence? On the absurdity of oversized ambitions? On the fallibility of great minds? Was the Underwear Incident a serendipitous occurrence that just happened, thanks to some bizarre concatenation of coincidences, to take place here and now? Or was it the predetermined outcome of the intentional accumulation and intersection of our individual fates?

Alberto had lit a cigarette, perhaps as a savagely ironical, even if unintended, exegesis on my hyperactive imagination. He stood silently, watching me, as if in anticipation of some grand statement on the meaning of life. None was forthcoming, alas, at least not from me. A strong breeze blew, swirling up the dust and the dirt, and I had to shut my eyes for a second. When I opened them, the shorts were gone. I looked at Alberto quizzically and he immediately understood. He flicked the cigarette in the direction of a rose bush. There, entangled in the thorns, were the shorts. Unnerved by this poetic reference to the Crucifixion, I rubbed my eyes and grabbed my suitcases. Alberto was smiling broadly and pointing at the bush.

"Eh, *signore,*" he said, "you want?" I shook my head. "Ardora Howze nice, *si*?" I nodded. "I theenk we gonna rock around clock tonight, no?"

I headed for the villa. Whatever the meaning of the Underwear Incident, it was an unsettling and portentous start to the gathering. Whether it boded good or ill I didn't know, but at a minimum I was glad to be rid of Alberto's company.

"*Arrivederci, signore!*" he shouted.

"And it's not Celentano," I yelled back. "It's Bill Haley and the Comets!"

TWO

C. Milosz has a portentous dream, survives two tremors, appreciates Mister Moto's genius, and has a major epiphany

I distinctly remember dreaming of a *ménage à trois* with Ada, Lolita, and the decidedly overtaxed—and sadly underperforming—Pnin (an unfortunate name that invariably reminds me of a sneeze: Pnin! Gesundheit!), when a loud bang similar to a thunderclap awoke me. The moon poured a silvery liquid into my room. I waded through the light and opened the window to see if it was raining, but the sky was icy and the firmament pulsated with the indifferent light of the receding stars. The cypresses appeared to stand at attention. Only the ticking of my alarm clock intruded on the serenity of the moment. The thunderclap, I decided, must have been some sort of freak weather phenomenon. We were in a lake region and tall mountains surrounded us on all sides. The atmosphere was liable to play all manner of tricks on us humans. Or was it a sonic boom?

And then it happened again. But this time the bang was accompanied by unmistakable tremors. The windowpanes rattled, a pen rolled off my night table, and I—that is to say, my body—shook. This was no thunderclap. This was, presumably, an earthquake. I had never experienced one before, but I knew one was supposed to exit buildings as quickly as possible. I donned my jeans, a clean shirt, and sandals—one of the unexpected advantages of sleeping in the nude is that dressing does not entail undressing—grabbed my laptop and four remaining copies of *First Things Last*, ran down the spiral staircase, and stumbled onto the illuminated lime lawn that sloped down to the slate-black lake. A few dozen people were already there, some in underwear, some in bathrobes, some in pajamas. A siren had gone off in the distance and the town glowed eerily. Moths circled the lamps like hostile redskins in cheap Hollywood Westerns.

"Not to worry, ladies and gentlemen, not to worry," one of the villa's personnel said. "This is a common occurrence in this part of Italy. Just a few slight tremors, that's all. They come and go. Nothing to worry about, I can assure you, nothing at all." We could hear a slight laugh. "You might say that the bark is far worse than the bite."

"Was that an earthquake?" someone asked. "I've never experienced an earthquake. Is that all there is to it?"

"Just a tremor, ladies and gentlemen, just a tremor. Happens all the time. Nothing to worry about. Ah, I see the waiters are bringing the brandy! How about a nice nightcap before we return to our rooms?"

When I deposited myself in bed an hour later, I tried to conjure up Ada, Lolita, and Anna Karenina, but to no avail. Was Pnin immersed in Anna? As far as I can recall, I slept soundly until eight.

***

After parting with Alberto the day before, I had followed the red-brick path that snaked to the villa. The smell of roses, intermingled with the maniacal clicking of the cicadas and the unrelenting glare of the cadmium-orange sun, was oppressive and I dove into the air-conditioned reception area, dumped my bags, and took a deep breath before proceeding to the desk with all the swagger I could muster. I could feel large round drops of sweat millimetering (a neologism!) their way down my back. The gum-chewing brunette greeted me with a formal smile that revealed painfully white incisors. Welcome to Ardor Haus, she said. How was I? I was fine. Was my trip comfortable? Yes, it was, thank you. She hoped my stay at the villa would be memorable. I was sure it would be. Would I mind registering and providing my credit card number, for incidentals? No, I would not. Would I like a wake-up call in the morning? Not necessary.

"Thank you very much, Professor Milosz," she concluded the ritual. "May I ask you, um, something? How do you pronounce your, um, first name?"

"Chester."

"Chester?"

"Yes, Chester."

"So the l is pronounced as a t? And the w as an r?"

"I beg your pardon?"

"I guess it's a poet thing, right?" She smiled sweetly as if commiserating with the odd quirks and bizarre foibles of my profession. "Oh, and here's an, um, information packet."

I needed a shower and a rest. "I guess it is," I replied and left for my room on the second floor. As I glanced down at her from the red-carpeted staircase, she waved merrily to me.

"Hope you win another NO-bell!" she chimed.

***

There were no events scheduled for the rest of the day, so, after taking a shower and a short nap, I resolved to explore the grounds and risk a quick foray into Caravaggio itself, before the natives got restless. Such gatherings tended to monopolize all one's time and, if I didn't take advantage of my freedom today, I might not have another opportunity later. The sun had already begun its descent toward the Occident and the heat had palpably abated, so I slipped on a pair of white cotton slacks, a black T-shirt, and an off-white cotton jacket. After all, when in Caravaggio, do as the Caravaggians do.

The villa was located on one side of a promontory that jutted out into the metallic lake, named, as one of the brochures in the information packet informed me, after the town, which was named after a millionaire industrialist who committed suicide in protest against Mussolini's discriminatory taxation policies. He took his yacht to the middle of the lake and then, his pockets laden with gold bullion, jumped into his watery grave. If you faced the hilly tip, the town was to your left and a dock with several rowboats was at the bottom of a sloping hill to your right. What may have been a ferry shimmered in the distance. A motor boat buzzed out from behind the cypresses and dashed across the coal-blue water. A wind-surfer turned over in the wake and the rowboats knocked against the dock. Alberto's intuition that "we're gonna rock around the clock tonight" came to mind (thereby demonstrating how easily errant sounds and smells can prompt sweet memories: were we not, after all, just prisoners of randomness and serendipity?). The cicadas clicked as before—with the same intensity and the same monotony—and the smell of the roses was still overpowering, but this time I drank them in. I turned toward the dock. It had been years since I had been in a rowboat. I would take a spin around the promontory and disembark in town, have a bite, and then return, just in time to fall, exhausted, I hoped, into bed.

As I was maneuvering the oars into the sockets, I heard a male voice: "Hullo! I say, mind if I join you?" It was a thin, silver-haired man of about sixty-five. His face was rectangular, his jaw was square, and his brown eyes had a doe-like quality that probably appealed to women, especially of an intellectual bent. The words "ruggedly handsome" fit him perfectly. He was dressed in moccasins, lime-green shorts, and a striped blue-and-red Polo shirt with upturned collar. Reluctantly, unwillingly, but politely (we are all prisoners of society), I spread my hands to signal assent. "Please," I said. "I'd be delighted."

"Dickey Lemon," he grinned, "billionaire extraordinaire." His long fingers encompassed my hand. "And you must be our Nobel prize-winning poet."

"Well," I blushed, "not quite."

"Don't be so modest, my dear chap. Never pays. Especially in my line of things. Though, I dare say, in no line of things. Even in the poetry business. And poetry is a bloody business, like show business, I guess." He grabbed a cushion and shoved it beneath his posterior. "No use for modesty, you know. Doesn't pay, doesn't get you the girl; doesn't even get you the ugly girl. Doesn't even get you the fat and ugly girl. Nice day, what? I say, maybe we should shove off?"

"And what is your line of things, Mister—?"

"Dickey. Call me Dickey, ole boy, just plain, ole Dickey. Dickey to my friends, Dickey to my enemies, Dickey to the world."

"So what is your line of things, Dickey?"

"Bloody hamsters."

"Hamsters? I don't quite understand."

"Know how many hamsters there are in the UK, ole boy? Millions. Know how many hamster cages there are in the UK? Bloody millions. Know how much the hamster bedding business is worth?"

"Hamster betting? I'm afraid I don't follow. Wouldn't you need a racetrack?"

"Oh, how droll! You mean betting—as with the ponies—don't you? Not very practical, I'm afraid. Awfully undisciplined little buggers—hamsters. Congenitally incapable of running in a straight line. Will think about it, though. Could be a gold mine. No," Dickey corrected me, "that was bedding—with two ds. The stuff they line the cages with." His aplomb, in all its high-calorie splendor, was fully on display. "Hullo! Know how much it's worth—per annum?"

"No." I was hopelessly out of my depth. "A few hundred thousand dollars?"

Dickey giggled. "More like five hundred million, ole boy," he said with the authority of a billionaire extraordinaire, "and I mean pounds." He beamed, as if waiting for me to say something. "And guess who owns it all?" The question, I suspected, was rhetorical.

"You?"

"Quite: Dickey Lemon, billionaire extraordinaire, at your service. Hullo!"

We had just managed to exit the little cove with the dock and were now on the open waters of Lake Caravaggio. The sky was still a brilliant blue. Outlined against the luxuriantly green promontory, the villa had turned a rusty golden color that made the white columns stand out and almost quiver. The shadows had lengthened and the cicadas appeared to have vanished. The only sound I could hear was the slapping of the waves against the sides of the boat—and Dickey's monologue. He explained how he got into the hamster bedding trade. He'd always liked the animals, even had a few as a child, but it was only after he'd acquired an M.B.A. from Oxford that it occurred to him that hamsters were a gold mine. Hamster owners generally lined cages with long strips of newspaper. That was fine, if a bit of a bother, as long as newspapers were the thing, but what would people do with the onset of the Internet and the death of print and globalization? Dickey was the first to catch that wave and, by offering his customers a variety of subtly different beddings every few months—"scent's the thing: housewives love it"—was able to capture the market.

"They call me the Hamster King, you know." His back stiffened slightly. "Anyway, what's the bloody point of having bloody billions if the world is going to bloody hell? Must do something, no? Can't just sit on my bank accounts, right? Social conscience, social responsibility, humanism, philanthropy, saving the world, and all that." He took a deep breath. "Not a bad thing, actually. Even profitable, bloody hell." Another breath and then the finale: "So here I am."

In between pulls on the oars, I nodded. The breeze felt like cream and I noticed that, if I ignored the content of Dickey's remarks, the singsong of his voice merged nicely with the percussive lapping of the waves to form a kind of odd jazz.

"Damned fine weather we're having," he continued. "Makes the ole brain cells go clickety-clack, clickety-clack. So tell me, Chess-law—"

"It's Chester."

"You pronounce it Chester?" He looked genuinely surprised. "Odd. Then why do you spell it Chess-law? Oh, well, your God-given right, I suppose. Free country, democracy, God save the Queen, liberalism, and all that. Made us great. Hell, made me a bloody billionaire! So tell me"—he looked me in the eyes—"Chess-TER: what's the answer? What's the bloody answer? If the politicos don't know, if the businessmen don't know, then you poets bloody better well know!"

"Well, I suppose it depends on what the question—"

"Genius! Bloody genius! Exactly what Joe says!"

"I beg your pardon? Joe who?"

"Zsasz"—he pronounced it Zass—"Joe Zsasz, the brains behind this show."

"I thought you were the brains."

"Did you? Did you now? That's bloody good, that's bloody damned bloody good! No, Chester, Mister Moneybags—that's me. Mister Brains—that's Joe. Smart chap, Joe. They say he's a genius. Not sure about that, but his head's screwed on right. Not a single nigger in the whole woodpile, if you know what I mean. Knows the right questions, Joe does." Dickey's voice trailed off, as if he had just remembered a pleasant memory.

"And you know the right answers?" I said hopefully.

"Do I? Do I? Wish I did, ole chap, sure as bloody hell wish I did." Once again, his voice trailed off and it was clear that Dickey's heart was no longer in the conversation. "I say, bloody nice weather. Couldn't be better. Not like merry ole England. Used to be a great country, right? Quite. Now, hullo! Nigger in every woodpile." He appeared distracted. "What say we have a drink or two?"

We had rounded the tip of the promontory and were within some one hundred yards of a narrow beach and a promenade that curved into town. Amid a cluster of palm trees stood a small bar with a striped red-and-green awning and several, mostly empty, tables. Dickey was right about the weather. The breeze on the lake had picked up, but it nicely balanced the expanding fatigue in my overheated arms and torso. I turned left and, a few minutes later, the boat cut through the pebbles with an extended groan and came to a sudden halt. I rose to my feet slowly and gingerly set one foot, and then another, into the smoothly rounded stones. Dickey almost stumbled, but, after regaining his balance and composure, he followed me to the café.

"A double Bombay martini, extra dry, two olives," he said with a tone of familiarity to the bartender. "And for my friend?"

"A beer," I said, "Moretti."

Two tables away from us sat a middle-aged couple. He was wearing a Panama hat, Seersucker suit, and ascot. She had pearl earrings, a pearl necklace, and a linen Coco Chanel suit. They were drinking Campari and staring silently at the lake. She crossed her legs. He raised his hand to his mouth and coughed discreetly. Our drinks arrived.

"Tell me more about Joe Zsasz."

"A genius, a bloody genius," Dickey remarked with renewed vigor. The martini had given him a shot of adrenaline and revived his spirits. "The brains behind this bloody show. The brains behind every show, I dare say."

"But who is he? I'm afraid I've never heard of him."

"You haven't? Bloody odd, that. Hullo! Everyone knows Joe. The Pope knows Joe. Wall Street knows Joe. The Queen knows Joe. Hell, bloody Hollywood knows Joe. Poet, right? In your own world, I guess. Nothing but words. Never cared for the stuff myself, I dare say. A thousand apologies and all that. Dickey Lemon, straight shooter, eh? Excellent martini, by the way. Good olives, too. The key to a good martini, by the way. Bloody hell! Good gin's always good, right? So it's all up to the olives, what?" Dickey placed the empty glass on the table and, with a slow circular turn of his hand, motioned to the bartender for another.

"Born in Hungary or Poland or CzechosloVAYkia or someplace like that. Never could get those countries straight. Too many of them. And too bloody small. Shouldn't Slovenia and Slovakia just drop the bloody pretense and be one country? Bloody hell! Sure, sure, national liberation, freedom of choice, and all that. Nothing to be done, I suppose. The Zeit-bloody-geist." He pierced an olive with a toothpick and removed it with his perfectly white teeth. "Father's a lawyer, mother's a do-gooder. Joe's the precocious son. Darling of mummy and daddy. University, law degree, sky's the limit, future's bright, onward and upward, and all that. What could go wrong? Bloody war is what. Adolf's boys lock up young Joe for something or other. A stint in Auschwitz, the good part, with the brick barracks. Then Stalin's boys show up. Mummy and daddy say go west, young man. But Joe stays, signs up with the NKV-bloody-D or something like that. Not the hundred-percent thugs, mind you, but the fifty-percent ones, the agitprop boys. Climbs the ladder, all's going well. Sky's the limit once again. Then Uncle Joe heads for eternity and Joe takes mummy and daddy's advice and goes west. Works his way up. Advisor, consultant, expert, and all that. When Joe talks, the world listens—with perked bloody ears. Top gun now. Bloody won some bloody genius prize: the McCarthy, McCarver, or something like that. Up to his neck in the green stuff. Politicians, big-money types with sundry skeletons and dirty laundry—and image problems. When Joe Zsasz talks, everybody listens. Hullo! Already said that, didn't I?" Dickey fished out the other olive with his fingers. "And here we are."

"In Caravaggio," I added.

"Bloody nice weather," Dickey said. He placed some large bills on the tabletop. "Should do it. What say we walk back? Tired of that bloody boat. Too much flapping. Like a ladies' bake sale. And not a single bloody gull. Ever been to Mousehole? Bloody beautiful country—Cornwall. Gulls galore, if you know what I mean. And"—Dickey winked—"not a single nigger in the woodpile." He cracked his knuckles and rose to his feet. "Good chinwag: deepest gratitude and felicitations and all that. Must do it again, what? Soon."

***

The alarm rang at eight, which was fortunate, as I had just begun dreaming of a potentially alarming liaison between Madame Bovary and Pnin. Why was that damned Pnin continually inserting himself, like a pneumatic drill, into my nocturnal treks? The connection with Nabokov and Ardor Haus was obvious, but there had to be more. Why not Van Veen? Or Humbert? Why an old, washed-out Russian émigré professor who lived in the past and yearned for Mother Russia's birch trees, endless snow, and relentless mud? Was my subconscious trying to tell me something about myself? Or was it a warning? And why did Pnin come to mind before and after an earthquake? I yawned and went to the window. The sky was painfully blue again. It would be another hot day. Fortunately, having kept Bacchus at arm's length, I had no hangover.

I surveyed my room for signs of damage from the tremors. A porcelain ashtray depicting Leda and the swan had slid to the very edge of the round table that stood in one corner. An open bottle of Pellegrino had tipped over and its contents had spilled onto the marble floor. The pictures—mostly cheap prints of Italian landscapes and Roman ruins—hung crookedly on the walls and I adjusted them. Otherwise, there were no cracks, no holes, no chipped plaster or paint. Had I really rushed out to the lawn in the middle of the night? Had there really been an earthquake? I turned on the faucets and stepped into the shower. A liquid-soap dispenser was attached to the tiles. Evidently, Ardor Haus didn't trust its guests with little bars of soap. But it did provide a hair dryer, a cotton bathrobe, and flimsy slippers in a crinkly cellophane wrapper.

Dickey waved enthusiastically as I arrived in the Otto Room for breakfast and, although I would have preferred dining alone, I had no choice but to join him and his dark-haired companion. Dickey was dressed impeccably: tan slacks, dark-red penny loafers, a white button-down cotton shirt, and a navy-blue jacket with a golden anchor embossed on the breast pocket. His friend looked well over sixty-five, wore thick glasses resting on a round-tipped nose, and had a scruffy mustache that extended far over his upper lip. He was smoking a thin black cigarillo, even though No Smoking signs hung prominently on all the walls.

"Come join us," Dickey bubbled. "Just finished briefing Joe about our little pow-wow yesterday. Questions, answers, and all that. Poetry and policy. Saving the world. Big job, right? Meet our chief of chiefs."

"Chess-wow," Joe radiated genuine delight. "Pull up chair. Have some brake-fest." He spoke with a thick Eastern European accent, not unlike Granddad's.

"Thank you," I said. "But it's Chester actually." A modest grin, almost apologetic.

"Amerikah-nee-ZAY-shun?" Joe took a pull on his cigarillo and laughed. "Great cown-tree, I know, I know."

"First impressions, ole boy?" Dickey piped in. "Bloody nice weather again, eh?"

"Well, the tremors were unexpected—and a bit terrifying." Another modest grin, but with no trace of apology.

"Like life," Joe sighed. "Irrt-quake eez like life."

"Well put, Joe," Dickey said, "well put. Bravo, maestro!" He turned to me. "The ole boy is really something, eh?" Then he turned back to Joe. "What's that you said about the economy, Joe? Just before our friend popped in?"

"Zere eez a my-cro and a mah-cro economy," Joe intoned.

"Bloody well said, Joe, bloody well said. Hit the nail on the head! As usual!" Dickey turned to me again. "Know why I'm the Hamster King, Chet? Because this man"—he placed his graceful hand on Joe's forearm—"is my guru."

A waiter poured me some coffee and I excused myself to go to the buffet. "Un-for-tue-net-ly," Joe said, "we too must go."

"Must start on time, eh?" Dickey added. "By the way, ole boy, see the brunette in the red dress and torpedo bra?" He nodded in the direction of the dessert table. "That's Louise Babylon. Quite a girl. Up your alley, I should think. Likes to spread the wealth around, if you know what I mean. Very generously—like the Queen of Sheba. Coffee's good, what? A shot in the bloody arm, eh? Ah, Louise, Louise! Been around the proverbial block a few times. Broken in quite a few ponies. Conference slut, right?" At just that moment, the object of his commentary turned and, seeing Dickey, smiled. "Bloody hell," he murmured, "here comes the bitch."

"Dickey!" she squealed. (Note how nicely the verb resonates with Dickey's commercial interests.)

"Louise, my pet!" Dickey said with a forced smile. His insouciance had evaporated like the morning dew. "Would love to chat, ole girl. But, but, but: must run, must run, must run." Was he nervous? Yes, he was. "What a day! What a life! You know, my love, the conference, the geniuses, and all that. Louise darling, meet my old friend Chet My-losh." And Dickey turned on his heels and, like his insouciance, disappeared.

"*Quel idiot*," she said sharply, obviously brooking no disagreement. (Why did she say it in French? Initially, I saw it as nothing more than a cloying affectation; eventually, I realized that *idiot* wasn't just an idiot. But more on that later.)

Louise had closely spaced brown eyes, full red lips made redder by liberal applications of some gloss, a thin nose that sustained old-fashioned horn-rimmed bifocals, and barely visible crow's feet masked by a crusty layer of face powder. Her rocket-like bosom looked nothing short of gargantuan, especially within the minimal confines of her flimsy silk dress. Her legs were the youngest part of her body and they stood in stiletto heels. No policymaker or businesswoman would dress like this. She had to be a journalist or, more likely, an intellectual, and a very fashionable one at that. Either way, I was in no mood for an extended encounter with another force of nature this early in the morning.

"Excuse my manners," I explained, "but I need to do some work in my room."

"Manners!" she snorted. "You poets get me, you really get me. Manners! Sure, go, what the hell. Manners!" She snorted again. "But sit next to me later. You may be the only barely tolerable person here." Another snort, intermingled with a prolonged giggle, followed. "Manners!" And then she swished back to the dessert table.

I made the proverbial dash for the exit. As I was turning the key to my door, my stomach produced a loud growl—fortunately, there was no one to hear it—and I realized I hadn't had any breakfast. I washed my hands and face—it was, I realized, a kind of ritual purification—donned my jacket, inserted a pen into the inside pocket, crept down the curved staircase, ran up the curved path to the main gate, and escaped into a café a few houses on the right. The bald bartender was reading a newspaper and smoking. He looked at me sleepily and smacked his enervated lips, as I ordered a double espresso *corretto* grappa. A fly crawled across the counter and, just before it reached the sugar container, paused, as if contemplating life's few alternatives, and then flew away. An old brass-colored radio with a huge dial was playing. After the announcer finished providing what appeared to be last day's sports scores, there followed the unmistakable voice of Adriano Celentano. Where was Alberto? Probably doing hairpin turns at one hundred forty. Where was I? About to experience the irrepressible Louise Babylon. I decided I'd prefer to be with the gentle Alberto in an out-of-control automobile in the Italian Alps. I finished the coffee and, in his memory, ordered another double espresso *corretto* grappa.

***

The proceedings were to be held in the Nikolai Room, named, I imagined, after Otto Nabokov's father. As was typical for these kinds of affairs, four long tables, with stiff white tablecloths that extended to the floor and hid legs, feet, and thighs, were arranged in a square. Microphones, bottles of Pellegrino, Coca-Cola, and Fanta, stacks of plastic cups, and little bowls of candy were positioned on the flat surface like watch towers in some Siberian gulag. Before each chair was a yellow ruled pad (legal size) and two neatly sharpened pencils. Joe Zsasz and Dickey Lemon were conferring before a wavy white screen. There would, evidently, be slides or a film. Some of the great minds had already assembled. Louise Babylon was seated with her back to the glass doors that opened onto the lawns. Smart, I thought. She knows that propinquity to an exit is a *sine qua non* of successful conferencing. And, more impressive, she knows one should never sit facing the light. She beckoned to me lazily with a long finger and pointed pointedly (forgive me, but I couldn't resist, this being about Louise) to the seat to her left.

"How was the chocolate cake?" I had noticed a smudge in the corner of her mouth.

"Don't be insufferable and sit down," she snapped and extended the tip of her tongue. "Which side?"

"Left." With a snake-like jab, she removed the impious chocolate.

"*Merci.*" A semi-snap followed by the trace of a smile.

"No problem."

"No problem! He says. Who speaks that way? What are you—

fifteen? Don't be insufferable and sit down." She poured herself some mineral water. "So what is it like being a world-famous poet? I bet you get all the girls."

"Well, I wouldn't say that," I replied feebly, sensing that I was turning crimson.

"All the boys?" A noticeable curl in the formerly smudged left corner of her mouth.

"No, no"—I felt completely off-guard—"no, not at all." She looked at me closely through her glasses.

"Funny, but I always thought you'd be older and had an accent."

"Because of the name? Actually, I pronounce it Millis."

"Millis? So I've been mispronouncing it all these years?" She produced a throaty laugh, akin to what you'd expect from a cheap Parisian chanteuse in interwar Belleville.

"All these years?" I said. "You flatter me."

"Don't be naïve," she reprimanded me sternly, her brow knotted. "As if you didn't know you're a world-famous poet."

"Well, thank you then."

"False modesty is infuriating, so stop," she ordered in the manner of a punctilious grade-school principal. "Look: the show is about to begin."

The entire group had assembled. Most were drinking coffee from Styrofoam cups and munching on croissants, muffins, or triangular pieces of baklava. Dickey was playing with the switch on his microphone, while Joe was shuffling through a pile of papers. A waiter was hurriedly removing some of the debris from the tables. Dickey gave me a thumbs-up sign. I returned it. Joe cleared his throat and slid the microphone toward himself.

"Good mor-neenk," he said, "velcome, lay-dees and gennelmens, to Ardor Haus."

Louise poked me in the ribs. "Wake me up when he's finished." I was going to poke her back, but decided not to, lest my elbow missed its intended target and grazed a breast. I had no idea what that might provoke, but instinctively realized that ignorance was indeed a blissful state. Joe proceeded to explain the origins and purpose of this grand undertaking, went on and on about extraordinarily great minds and the extraordinary challenge of an extraordinarily globalized world, thanked Dickey profusely, if somewhat tight-lippedly, for his foresight, support, and generosity—Dickey lowered his eyes modestly as he did—thanked Malvina Florentina, the extraordinary Ardor Haus director, for her foresight, support, and generosity—Florentina, a stunning blonde who looked exactly like the young Monica Vitti, did not lower her eyes modestly—and then continued with thickly accented and virtually incomprehensible one-line introductions of all the attendees. "You all know who you are," he said unhelpfully, released a loud sigh, and, like a runner in a relay race, passed the microphone to Dickey.

"Who are these people?" I whispered to Louise. If anyone would know, the "conference slut" would.

"You don't know?" She was incredulous. "Poets! And they say *we* live in an ivory tower." Dickey began his peroration. To my surprise, he was reading from a prepared text. It would be boilerplate and I decided to satisfy my curiosity at the fount of Professor Babylon's wisdom.

"Haven't a clue. Well, except for Dickey and Joe. And I think I've heard of Kriegman."

"He's the self-important little man with the face of a chipmunk—over there. You really don't know who he is?"

"Not a clue."

"Famous journalist, winner of five Pulitzers"—I confess to having cringed at the sound of that hated word—"author of a weekly column in all the newspapers of the world, darling of talk shows, quintessential white guy in tie, and author of the best-selling *The Moon Is Flat*." I nodded. "And," she ended with a fatal thrust and a savage glint, "a world-class jerk."

"You sound like you know him."

"We dated a few months." (Said grudgingly, almost as if it were a concession of strategically important territory to a savage foe.)

"But you just said he's a world-class jerk!"

"That was many years ago when he wasn't. Well, not a world-class jerk—just a jerk."

"Not the best of commentaries on your judgment, is it?"

"Don't be insufferable."

"So what is *The Moon Is Flat* about?"

"You know how they say globalization is flattening the world and making all of us part of one big global village? Well, Kriegman's arguing that globalization will now flatten the universe."

"All of it?" I couldn't hide my skepticism. "The universe is a pretty big place."

"Size is a social construction," she declared. Then she purred, "In most cases."

The audience began applauding and I turned to see Dickey smiling graciously. I gave him a thumbs-up sign and he immediately returned it. I would have to congratulate him on his brilliant introduction at lunch, which, according to my watch (a modest Casio, I might add, one that resembled a poor cousin of Louise's Zeiss or Dickey's Rolex), should be in about an hour on the patio. "Guess who's next?" Louise said. The little red light on Kriegman's microphone was shining. He held it in his right hand, as if it were an axe, and brought it within inches of his mouth.

"The moon is flat." He spoke in a slow, ponderous, and portentous monotone. "So what? You say. So everything, I tell you."

Louise groaned, a bit more audibly than the confined space graciously permitted. "There he goes again. He's been saying everything is flat for the past twenty years."

I saw my chance. "Including you?" She rolled her eyes.

"As Ralph Kramden used to say, 'you're a riot, Alice, a regular riot'."

"I beg your pardon?" This was, no doubt, a contemporary cultural reference and I was lost. Or was this Kramden a devotee of Virginia Wolf and Alice B. Toklas's Parisian salon? If so, I should have known his work and not knowing it distressed me—but only momentarily, until Louise resumed her charge.

"You mean to say you don't know who Ralph Kramden is? *Incroyable!* Where have you been all your life?" Then she sneered (this was a shocker: I don't think I've ever been sneered at): "Don't tell me: writing poetry in your room." Her voice rose. "Don't you ever go out?"

Kriegman paused in mid-sentence and glared in our direction. Had he overheard Louise? She didn't seem to care and stared back. I heard him say "But not as flat as a tire" and then pause for the giggles that the comparison provoked.

I reached for the Pellegrino, but, like the glassware in that fifties' movie about the Titanic, the bottle slid out of my reach and fell off the table. Coffee cups clattered and several empty bottles did a rumba and tipped over. The earth produced a thunderclap just as the astonished Kriegman yelled, "Earthquake!" and ran for the exit. "Well," Louise said, "at least we don't have to listen to him anymore." Someone screamed, Dickey looked confused, while Joe Zsasz spoke calmly into the microphone and urged us all to go outside as quickly as possible. "But, pleeze," he said, "no pah-neek."

Louise took my hand and we made for the glass door just behind us. Outside, the sky was its usual artificial blue. The cicadas were undeterred by the tremor and the cypresses resembled moving paintbrushes on an azure canvas. As that analogy occurred to me, I realized that, unlike the first time the tremors had struck, I felt no confusion and no panic whatsoever. Was that because poetry was a source, not only of truth, but also of spiritual fortitude? Louise's stilettos, meanwhile, had sunk into the moist earth and, after trying to regain her balance by waving her arms and extending one leg, she toppled over and fell face down into the grass. A series of exceptionally coarse expletives ensued and it dawned on me that this was as good a time as any to beat a retreat from her verbal assaults. Besides, she would be in an even viler mood when she got on her feet, the commotion would last another hour or so, and, in the meantime, I could have another espresso *corretto*, naturally, with grappa—or Sambuca—in the café near the gate.

***

Kriegman the peripatetic world traveler had beaten me to the establishment. Considering his mad dash out of the Nikolai Room, I shouldn't have been surprised to see him. It was too late and too awkward to withdraw, so I raised my eyebrows in greeting. He placed an empty glass on the bar and managed a constipated smile. His hand was trembling as he extended it to shake mine.

"Thor Kriegman," he sighed. "My friends call me Jake."

"Chester Milosz," I replied, "but I pronounce it Millis."

"Sure, whatever. Have a drink, on me."

"I'll have what you're having." It looked like scotch.

"On the rocks?"

"What else?" I replied. Kriegman rapped the bar and pointed at himself and me.

"*Due*. Scotch. *Con* rocks, OK?" The bartender nodded.

"Good talk," I said. "Too bad the tremor almost flattened the villa." Would he understand my feeble attempt at wordplay? If he did, he ignored it.

"It's the nature of the biz. Easy come, easy go. You win some, you lose some. Cheers! What should we drink to? I know: let's drink to Louise Babylon. She probably told you we used to date. Lemme tell you something, Chester: *that* was the biggest mistake of my life. The woman's neurotic, psychotic, bipolar, and everything in between and I'm glad I came out of that so-called relationship with my sanity and a shred of dignity intact. As to you, all I can say is: be careful. I saw her sizing you up like a famished tiger about to pounce on a mouse. She'll devour you, Chet. She'll eat you up and spit you out. And you'll wind up sitting in your own crap as she waltzes away with her next victim. You won't listen, of course. No one does. So here's what I suggest, Chester. Let's drink to you *and* Louise—a coupling made in hell." He raised his glass, but I immediately took a sip from mine.

"Tell me, Thor." It was too soon for Jake. "Who is La Babylon?" If anyone knew, Thor Kriegman did. "What is she doing here? The only person who's more out of place at this conference is me." I took another sip. "To tell you the truth, I don't much like her."

"With what astonishing celerity our newly established palness is evolving!" He downed the scotch and ordered another by twirling his hand. "Well, since we've begun trading girlish confidences, Chet, lemme tell you that I hated her the first time we met. I positively detested her. So I can't say I wasn't fully aware of what I eventually got myself into. My eyes, as they say, were shut wide open. What you think or think you think doesn't matter with La Babylon. That's a good one, by the way. What little Louise wants, little Louise gets. But you know that and it won't make an iota of a difference." He seemed distracted. "You wanted to know something else. Yes, right: who she is. Right? A distinguished Ivy League prof, writes for all the big academic journals no one reads. About what? Good question. I've never managed to get past the first paragraph, but it's always something about gender and civil society and globalization, etcetera, etcetera, and so on and so forth. The girl lives on the conference circuit: Paris, London, Rome, you name it. Speaks French, German, and a smattering of Italian—or is it Spanish? No matter, the boys love it when she coos to them in their native tongue. What else? Right! Vulgar as all hell: can make a dozen sailors blush. Oh, and this: I know from personal experience that she could subsist on chocolate cake."

"You've just described half my colleagues," I remarked with what I hoped was the appropriate degree of dryness and cool.

"So why is she at the renowned Ardor Haus hobnobbing with the world's movers and shakers and doers? That's what you want to know, right? Simple, Chet. I'm not the only one she's had in her talons. The esteemed Mister Lemon, the distinguished Doctor Zsasz are two other victims, at least as far as I know." His voice turned bitter. "I bet she's cavorted with the whole lot—except for you, that is."

"You still love her." I was, frankly, taken aback by my own perspicacity and boldness.

"Yes and no and no and yes, Chet. Actually, I detest the bitch. I detest every bone in her body. But, as La Babylon never tires of saying, the opposite of love isn't hatred. It's indifference. Another drink? For the road?" It was time to go, if only because I'd have to carry Kriegman if he had another scotch.

"We should be getting back," I opined. "They'll be wondering where their guest speaker is."

"Right!" he exclaimed and placed a few bills on the bar. "What do you think of *The Moon Is Flat*? Clever title, no? It's sold millions." We stepped outside and I took Kriegman by the arm and led him to the gate. "You know what my next book will be called? *The Sun Is Flat*. Clever, no? Did you know my competition at the *New York Times* was approached by the Flat Earth Society? They wanted him to be their honorary president." He giggled. "I bet he agreed."

***

The smiling girl at the reception desk told us the others were having lunch on the patio near the rose garden. Was there any damage from the tremor? No, *va bene, va bene. Tutto*? *Tutto*. Absolutely *tutto*? *Si*, absolutely. Her eyelashes fluttered as Kriegman stroked her cheek. *"Mucho bella,"* he said. "You're very beautiful." *Grazie*, she lowered her eyes and flushed. I pulled at his arm. "Let's get something to eat, Thor. I'm starved." *"Mucho, mucho bella,"* he mumbled as I dragged him away.

"Hullo! Thor! Chester! So glad to see you!" It was Dickey. "Have a drink? Bloody earthquake that bloody never was, what? But what a panic, eh? Fear of God, impending mortality, the human condition, and all that. But, *que sera, sera*, I suppose. Still, a bloody unnecessary fright. Gets the ole adrenalin running and the ole ticker pumping a jot too fast, eh? Splendid spread, by the way. Caviar, lobster, oysters—and bottles and bottles of the very best bubbly. The perfect host, that Joe, what? Perfect weather, too. Except for that bloody quake. Have a bite."

"I think I'll have the champagne," Kriegman said and headed for the bar.

"Brilliant chap," Dickey observed. "Top notch, top gun, top of the line, top of the shelf. Hobnobs with the powerful and mighty, Thor does. He talks, they listen. Been everywhere, done everything. Damned lucky we got him. Insists on being called Jake, though. Never could understand that. Quirky journalist, what? Like you poets, eh? Damned lucky we bloody got him. Thank Joe for that. Ah, speak of the devil!"

Joe Zsasz approached us with a plateful of plump oysters on

a half shell in one hand and a flute of champagne in the other. His eyes were glowing like two moons.

"You should write po-yem about our mee-teenk."

"I'm sure I will."

"Good mee-teenk so far." Joe's voice, like that of a Valley Girl, turned quizzical toward the end of the sentence. Was that a question or an observation? "Very good mee-teenk." This time it was obviously an observation.

"Except for the tremor," I said. "Twice in one day. That can't be normal, can it?"

"What eez nor-mahl?"

"Spot on, Joe! Hit the nail on the head again!" Dickey interjected. "Told you, Chet: the man's a bloody genius."

"But two tremors a few hours apart," I objected. "Aren't you worried?"

"A whisper in the howl of history! Right, Joe? A bloody whisper in the bloody howl of history! That's what they were. Bit of a fright, but nothing to worry about. A bloody whisper in the bloody howl of bloody history. Here today, gone tomorrow, and all that. The transience of life, what? Easy come, easy go—easy bloody come, easy bloody go."

Dickey's bravado was clearly for show, but I liked that phrase—a whisper in the howl of history. It had a ring to it. And it was smart, damned smart, almost in a Nabokovian kind of way. The contrast between whisper and howl, the sibilance and the alliteration, and the final homage that the contrast paid to memory, to the past that made the present and the future possible, if not inevitable, appealed to me. Just how Dickey managed to string together these Homeric words I couldn't fathom and whether or not he was even aware of the mythic depth of his utterance I didn't know. In any case, I would have to use the phrase as a title. For a poem? Not quite my style. For my memoirs? Not bad. For my speech in Oslo? Not bad at all. I grabbed a napkin from a passing waiter and jotted down the phrase. I had the perfect opening: "Your Excellency, esteemed members of the Nobel Prize committee, ladies and gentlemen, [pause] my presence here today is a whisper [pause] in the howl of [pause] history."

"Ah," Joe observed, "I see cree-AH-teeve process never sleeps. Bon ah-peh-teet, Chess-wow. Come, DEE-kee, vee must talk."

They wandered off to a side table, sat down, and hunched over conspiratorially. I fought my way through the obstreperous crowd toward the buffet. Everyone's plate appeared distressingly full and, as I feared, by the time I reached the long table manned by two impassive waiters in fluffy chef's hats, the trays were bare, except for a weather-beaten shrimp and several bowls of mostly crushed oyster crackers. The shrimp looked suspicious, so I took a handful of crackers and cracker debris and stuffed them into my mouth. The champagne was also gone, so I grabbed a bottle of warm Coke and drank it greedily. After my encounter with Kriegman, I should've known it'd be flat. As I reached for more crackers, I felt a sharp poke in the small of my back.

"That's no way to treat a lady, buster." It was Louise Babylon, of course. "You could've helped me get up, you know. Or can't you get it up?"

"I had a long chat with your friend Kriegman." Ignore her, I ordered myself. I wasn't going to let myself be baited. "He still loves you," I said blandly.

"They all do," she smiled. "*Les idiots*. And what did he tell you about me?"

"Nothing," I smiled back, with the sweetness of cheap Marzipan. "He's planning to write a sequel."

"You didn't talk about me?" She sounded disappointed. "I don't believe it."

"Honest Injun," I said. And then a jab: "You seem to think you're more interesting than you are."

"Don't be insufferable," she said and walked away. Did she storm off? I wished that were the case, but I couldn't tell for sure. The bored expression on her face hadn't changed, her nostrils didn't flare, her breathing hadn't quickened. Every poetic bone in my body wished that she had stormed off—in a proverbial huff, no less!—but I had to settle for merely walked away. Too bad. My prose could use some drama. Well, there was no point crying over unspilled milk. But at least I had drawn blood and she now knew that the Honorable Chester Milosz was no pushover. I emptied the bowl and popped three crackers into my mouth.

On the way out, I leaned over and whispered into Dickey's ear: "My apologies, but I may have to miss the next session. I need to lie down." He looked alarmed.

"Nothing serious, ole boy?"

"Just a bad oyster," I said.

"Bloody hell!"

"Not to worry." I tapped him on the back. "See you in a bit." My plan was simple. I'd have a meal in town and then return with the rowboat. If I timed it right, I'd be back for dinner.

***

The Wu-Fu Palazzo Chinese restaurant was irresistible. The food would be about as American as anything I could get back home and, despite my grandiose ambitions, I was sorely in need of a touch of the familiar. I decided to pass on the "fried rice with crap meat" and, perhaps predictably in light of my missed opportunities at the buffet, opted for the "noodle with shrimp."

"Noo-doe wi' shlimp," the waiter dutifully repeated. "Dlink? *Bevanda*?"

"Tea."

"One tea?"

"*Si*, one. And one spring roll, please."

"One spling loll?"

"Yes, one. *Grazie*."

"*Plego. Tutto*?"

"*Si, tutto*."

"OK, boss," the waiter began reading from his pad, "one nood-doe wi' shlimp, one tea, one spling loll. OK, boss?"

"OK."

Feeling slightly guilty about not correcting the waiter's unfortunate, even if unintentional, reinforcement of Orientalist linguistic stereotypes, I turned my gaze to a small pile of newspapers lying on a gilded table set against the crimson velour-draped wall to my right. The local rag had a screaming headline on the cover—TERREMOTO!—and a photograph of collapsed houses. There was no point in asking the waiter to explain what *terremoto* meant, so I rummaged through the pile and finally found a copy of today's *International Herald Tribune*. The page-one story in the upper-right hand corner read: "Monster Earthquake in Northern Italy: Hundreds Feared Dead." It registered 6.0 on the Richter scale and, as far as I could tell from the little map, its epicenter was about one or two hundred miles northeast of Caravaggio. Well, that explained the tremors. Several villages had apparently been turned to rubble. Two-hundred fifty-eight were confirmed dead and another seventy-seven were still missing. The Italian government had flown in aid and both the Europeans and the Americans had promised to send massive humanitarian assistance. The Pope would hold a special Mass. A right-wing politician averred that the calamity was an expression of God's wrath at the country's low birth rate. A communist warned that Uncle Sam's help always came with capitalist strings attached.

Terremoto: an odd word. I confess, shamefacedly, that I couldn't help but think of the diminutive Peter Lorre's Japanese detective, Mister Moto, who spoke impeccable English and always managed to outwit the blustering Americans with his keen sense for detail and his uncanny ability to flip substantially larger opponents and send them crashing into china cabinets. On the other hand, I took some pleasure from the evident fact that my poetic synapses were going, as Dickey Lemon might have put it, clickety-clack, clickety-clack. Would the *terremoto* also crack my writer's block? I didn't believe in heavenly signs, but the earthquake just might have been one. And then there was this unlikely memory of Mister Moto. Was I the target of intertextuality? Was my life—my creativity—about to experience a "flip" that would send it crashing, not into china cabinets, but into new realms of experience? I had, I realized, just used the word *experience* twice in one sentence. I never did that, neither in my prose, nor in my poetry. Did that stylistic lapse not portend a breakthrough? After all, wasn't a crash nothing but a breakthrough? And wouldn't that breakthrough end with my prize in Oslo? The food arrived, but, energized by this epiphany—there was no other word for the insights sparked by my contemplation of Mister Moto—I had suddenly lost my appetite and felt a pressing need for the wide expanse of the lake and sky. I fished out several coins—even in Europe, Chinese restaurants are notoriously inexpensive—and dropped them on the table.

"You no hungly?" The waiter looked disappointed. "Vely good."

"It looks wonderful, but I just realized I have an urgent appointment."

"Ulgent appointment," he repeated sadly. "OK, boss. Maybe you take?"

"*Grazie*, no, but"—and I snapped up a large shrimp resting atop the noodles—"I will have one for the road."

"OK, boss," he smiled, "noo-doe fo' me."

Someday, I resolved, I would have to come back and give him a lesson in proper English. And remind him that, if he ever expected his country to join the ranks of the civilized world, he'd have to look for linguistic inspiration to Mister Moto, and not the notorious Fu Manchu.

***

The rowboat was exactly where Dickey and I had left it the day before, looking as forlorn as a beached whale. The bartender in the café next door recognized me and waved lazily. "Dreenk?" he asked. His voice was unpleasantly high pitched. I was desperate to escape and, waving back, gave the boat a push and clambered in without getting my shoes wet.

I had run through town, trying to retrace, backwards, the route Dickey and I had followed. The ubiquitous tourists and the homogeneity of the souvenir shops led me to make a wrong turn and, after a few minutes, I realized I was lost in a labyrinth of narrow alleys that, regardless of which one I followed, always brought me back to my starting point.

"*Lago*?" I asked the stout proprietor of a small vegetable shop. "Where is the lake—*dove lago*?" He squinted and wiped his powerful hands in the soiled white apron he wore. I noticed he was wearing a hammer-and-sickle pin.

"*Là*," he pointed in some indeterminate direction. I bounded off like a stag, ran up and down several narrow stone steps, and, a little while later, espied his shop. When he saw me, he clucked in amusement and clapped his gnarled hands.

"*Vino*?" he asked. "*Eccellente*."

"No *vino*," I almost shouted, "I want *lago*!" I almost wilted from embarrassment upon hearing that absurd sentence echo in my mind.

"*Là, là*," he jabbed impatiently. "*Sempre dritto, sempre dritto*."

"Straight ahead?" I asked. "Did you say straight ahead?" Idiot! Without waiting for an answer, I squeezed into the only passageway that seemed to go straight ahead and several seconds later discovered that I had been going around in circles some fifty feet from the promenade. As the cool breeze of the lake caressed my sweaty face, I recalled that I might have heard the green grocer shout "*capitalista stupido*!" as I disappeared in the alley. No matter. I had wanted the *lago* and here it was, a dappled sheet of aluminum foil in all its tawdry glory.

Fortunately, the physical exertion of rowing against the waves quickly obliterated these memories. I was, finally, alone and completely sober. It was time for some serious stocktaking. Very well, I appeared to be on the brink of a major existential transformation. There was nothing to do about it except wait, patiently. It the transformation would come, it would come. My Muses were fickle beings who refused to be controlled by my whims. They too would come when they would come. Moreover, that brink had been sparked—not to worry: I was fully aware of the resounding awfulness of that mixed metaphor, but, considering what I had just been through, decided not to care—by my stay in Caravaggio, by my conversations with Dickey, Joe, Louise, and Thor, and, last but not least, by the *terremoto.* True enough, but what was the point of this gathering and why was I here? I hadn't noticed any attempt to identify, let alone solve, the world's problems. The foursome I had met were all distinguished—or more or less distinguished—in their own right, but they appeared to share few points of intersection, other than La Babylon's sexual favors.

Every text had a subtext and Ardor Haus was a text. It had to have a subtext, but what? For the first and only time in my life, I momentarily regretted not being a mystery writer. This was terrain that Agatha Christie and Eric Ambler were more suited to explore than Czesław Miłosz or Chester Milosz. And then the transparently obvious struck me. *They thought I was Czesław Miłosz!* They thought I was a Nobel Prize winner! Very well, I would play their game and see what happened. "See, Mister Moto?" I said out loud. "Your faithful pupil is learning from his master!" At that very moment, a large gull swooped past and emitted an extended caw. Was this a sign? One never knew, so, feeling both slightly ridiculous and fully empowered, I cried, "Thank you, Mister Moto, for your vote of confidence. I shall not disappoint you!" I noticed that I had reached the promontory and began rowing with renewed vigor.

As I approached the cove, I stopped rowing and swung the oars into the boat. The sun shone with its usual intensity and I lay back and closed my eyes. The waves lapped lazily against the sides of the boat. A woman's laugh carried across the water. The back of my eyelids was a dark orange. I shielded my eyes from the sun, inhaled deeply, and promptly fell asleep. Ada was regaling me with incomprehensible wordplay, while Lolita was tempting me with glimpses of her white ankle. Meanwhile, Vladimir Nabokov leaped into the air with his butterfly net and disappeared in the clouds. I was about to take the two girls by the hand and follow him when the sensation of falling abruptly roused me. As I came to, I realized it hadn't just been a dream. The boat had tilted dangerously to one side and I had slid against the cool oar. Two wet hands gripped the side, inches from my head. I steadied myself and looked into a woman's round Slavic face.

"A-lla Be-lo-mor-ka-nal-ska-ya," she said in between long breaths. "May I come on board?" Her English, amazingly, was accent free. "I have been swimming for an hour and feel very tired."

I pulled on her hands and she slithered into the boat like a python. Unlike most snakes, this one was wearing a maroon one-piece Spandex suit that did little to conceal her liquid breasts and opulent buttocks. She had long firm legs and long firm arms. The eyes were icy blue—careful, Chester, I thought, careful—and the hair was a shocking orange. She could've been a model. I had just introduced myself—gallantly, I might add—and was about to ask her who she was when she launched into an extended discourse.

Her name was unusual, but her grandfather had served as a supervisor on the White Sea Canal project and had received the moniker, Belomorkanalsky, from none other than Stalin himself. Knowing a good turn of events when he saw one, Papa formally changed his name during the Great Purges and, as he expected, not only survived, but survived in spades. Naturally, English speakers have difficulty pronouncing the name, but she didn't care and in time even came to appreciate that its complexity was unforgettable and could serve as a brand. Her own firm was named BMK Ltd. and Belomorkanalskaya was a real-estate magnate with vast holdings scattered throughout the former Soviet bloc. There were business centers in Warsaw, Prague, Bucharest, and Kyiv, sports stadiums in Donetsk, Yaroslavl, and Nizhni Novgorod, apartment complexes in Moscow, Saint Petersburg, and Vladivostok, and several brownfield developments in Luhansk and Sevastopol. She was thinking of getting into the energy business, she said, and was considering acquiring shares in a Liquefied Natural Gas terminal in Sochi and underground gas storage facilities in Ukraine, Slovakia, Estonia, and Kaliningrad. Needless to say, I was impressed, especially as her overpowering appearance needlessly, and cruelly, reinforced her status as one of Russia's richest and most powerful women. Where had she learned her English? Papa had been a high-ranking KGB officer stationed for over a decade in London. "I went to the best private schools, of course."

"You must be a friend of Dickey Lemon?" I asked.

"Oh, no," she said firmly, "Joe Zsasz."

"Joe really gets around."

"Joe is a player," she corrected me. "He is important—a V.I.P."

"Yes," I remarked, "I've come to appreciate that."

"And you are a poet." She sounded disappointed. "But at least you are a famous poet."

"I thought you Russians loved poets: Yevtushenko, Voznesensky, Pasternak, Akhmatova, Tsvetaeva…" I figured five would be enough to establish my credentials.

"When we were poor," she smiled (slyly and with a pinch of irony). "Now we prefer *das Kapital.*"

"Marx?" I was confused.

"Of course not," she snapped, but with far less vehemence than La Babylon. "Money." She looked around impatiently, as if waiting for someone. "Perhaps you could row more quickly? I need to take a bath before dinner. This water is filthy."

***

My head felt wooly and my feet were unresponsive as we climbed the path to the villa. Once in my room, I looked at myself in the oval mirror above the dresser and saw that my face and arms were sunburnt. A cold shower and several glasses of Pellegrino re-established some equilibrium, but the woolliness quickly returned and I knew I had to lie down. Dinner wasn't for another hour and, since it was going to be another buffet, I knew I could make a late appearance without drawing too much attention to my tardiness. Needless to say, I was wrong. (But, you might object, if it's truly needless, why am I saying it? Think about it and, as you do, remember: never trust a wordsmith!) When, two hours later, wearing a striped red-and-ochre Polo shirt, khaki shorts, and flip-flops, I shuffled down the staircase, feeling clear headed and fresh, and bounded into the Otto Room on my way to the patio where, I was certain, the buffet would be, I was shocked to see that the group, dressed in evening attire, was sitting at round tables and pecking at shrimp cocktails.

"Ah, Chess-wow!" Joe Zsasz cried as all heads turned toward me. "Our guest of hah-nor has finally come! Your seat eez zere—next to Jean-Pierre and my good friend, Sam." Joe rose to his feet and raised his glass. "Lay-dees and gennel-mens, a toast to po-yetry and to our great po-yet, Chess-wow!" Everyone applauded, while I turned to Jean-Pierre and Sam and whispered, "Actually, I prefer Chester."

THREE

C. Milosz watches a president descend from the heavens and swim like a dolphin, plays bocce ball, and takes a dramatic dip in the lake during a thunderstorm

The buffet had turned out to be a banquet, in my honor no less, but, after the initial *terremoto* I felt upon entering the Otto Room, things settled down and most of the evening went by uneventfully. At one point, Joe asked me to come to the podium and deliver a few words—which I did, with surprising ease. I wasn't quite dressed for the occasion (the understatement of the year, you might say), but, rather than apologizing for my appearance, I decided to follow in the intrepid Belomorkanalskaya's wet footsteps and turn a seeming debit into an asset. Heck, I thought: I was a Nobel Prize-winning poet and I could dress as a Nobel Prize-winning poet! I said something about how poetry could cure "captive minds" (I know: that bit was shameless) in the age of globalization, invoked the spirits of Homer, Shakespeare, Goethe, Pushkin, Shevchenko, and Frost, cited John Lennon, Arthur Rimbaud, and—why not? I was on a roll—Adriano Celentano, thanked the audience "from the depths of my lyrical heart" for this great honor, and expressed the certainty that we would "rock around the clock" tonight and every night. Unstoppable, I ended my speech with "Long live the spirit of Rimbaud!" I had no idea what that meant, but it seemed appropriate for the occasion. Thunderous applause followed. Glasses clinked. Eyes glowed. I returned to my table with a swagger like John Wayne's.

My immediate dinner companions were Jean-Pierre La Baguette and Samuel Livingston Roach. Across from us sat Serge Joupanencoff, Alexandra Wirrwarr, Ariadne Balletmeister, Emilia de Pouff, and Bogusława Wielkomała. Evidently, Dickey and Joe had decided to dispense with the usual boy-girl seating arrangement at such events. Rapid-fire introductions followed. La Baguette was a professor of history somewhere in western Canada. Roach was an international consultant. Joupanencoff was a film actor. Wirrwarr was deputy minister of something for some European government.

Balletmeister was in finance: did she say Frankfurt or did she say Singapore? De Pouff worked for some United Nations agency in Paris. And Wielkomała was in the IT business in Poland's very junior version of Silicon *Dolina*.

La Baguette was about sixty-five-seventy, bearded, husky, with a soft voice. The unfortunately named Roach couldn't have been over sixty: he had a large forehead, protruding ears, a thin nose, and thick glasses that magnified his eyes to terrifying proportions. The others were all in their forties. With his long blond hair and lime-green silk scarf, Joupanencoff gave the impression of desperately wanting to look like the actor he was. The ladies were all impeccably, and identically, dressed in serious suits and silk blouses. Wirrwarr wore her auburn hair in a tight bun accentuated by the heavy black frames of her designer glasses and cherry-red lips. Balletmeister's hair was cut short; her high cheekbones and pointed chin were set off against a surprisingly perky nose and a no-nonsense chin. De Pouff was the best looking of the lot, with an Audrey Hepburn neck and Elizabeth Taylor eyes. Need I say more? Wielkomała, like Belomorkanalskaya, looked very Slavic—round face, round eyes, round chin, and a round-tipped nose.

"Excellent speech," La Baguette said as I sat down. "I just loved your final line: Long live Rambo! It takes guts to place colonial violence and American imperialism at the core of the Western narrative from William Shakespeare to Sylvester Stallone."

"Uh, thank you." Mystification, a faux-knowing smile, and a resolution to change the subject as quickly as possible.

What did he study? I politely asked La Baguette. We academics usually coped with awkward conversations by asking that question. The history of history negationism, he said. Meaning what? The history of how history is negated, he answered. Denied? No, not denied, he sniffed, negated. As in what? I persisted. As in not being given its full due. Its full due as what? Its full due as the only narrative worth narrating and deconstructing. Hmm, so my poetry isn't worth narrating? Writing poetry, yes; narrating it, no. Then that leaves me in a pickle, doesn't it? Evidently. So what should I do? Become a historian of history negationism. I see. I'm glad you do, he said; most don't. Were you always a historian of history negationism? I asked. No, I had been in a seminary. But you lost your calling? No, God told me to... I interjected: to become a historian of negationism? Yes. Was he a friend of Joe Zsasz? A colleague. A colleague? Yes, they had common interests. In negationism? No, not in negationism. Then in what? Ah is all he said. I decided not to pursue my line of enquiry anymore.

Roach proved to be a less evasive conversationalist. He was currently on the payroll of the Fjord Motor Company, a Scandinavian outfit that, on his advice, produced mini-compacts and outsized sports utility vehicles, on the rationale that, if they could capture both ends of the global market, the middle would soon follow. Wasn't that the firm accused of supplying low-cost Land Rover knock-offs to terrorist regimes? A dirty lie perpetrated by Fjord's enemies. How could he be so sure? He had personally conducted a thorough investigation and uncovered no wrongdoing. But he was Fjord's consultant! So what? Well, wasn't there a conflict of interests? No. No? No. So what else did he do? He served on the boards of several Caribbean banks and international oil majors. Was he a friend of Joe Zsasz? No, he and Dickey had roomed together in college. Did he suspect then that Dickey would one day become the Hamster King? He turned away and poked the *steak au poivre* with his fork. Having lacked a solid meal in some twenty-four hours, I followed his example and devoured mine in hyena-like fashion in a few minutes.

"I understand now why they speak of starving poets." It was Wirrwarr, who sat opposite me and was cradling a wine glass in her hand. "You gave a very inspirational talk." Was she the deputy minister or the UN bigwig? The latter, I decided. "Would you like to speak to my people?"

"Your people?"

"Yes, my people. They need to hear a different perspective. They can be *so*"—she appeared to be searching for the perfect word—"provincial."

"I will be happy to speak to your people," I stated. "We poets belong to the world." That was a bit thick, but, after all, this was my party. "Poetry can change the world," I added solemnly. "Make poetry, not war."

"*Genau*," she exclaimed, "exactly." Ah, so Wirrwarr was German. "There are many in my party who would agree with what you just said. And there are many, alas, who would not." Was she Green? And did this mean she was the deputy minister? Yes, that must be it, I decided.

"I belong to the party of humanity," I intoned. "And I negate everything that negates humanity." I could see that La Baguette stopped chewing and glared at me from the corner of his eye.

"*Genau!*" she cried with even greater enthusiasm. "I, too, want to be a member of that party!"

This had gone far enough. I was tired and not a little overwhelmed with creeping rootlessness, but, as guest of honor, I couldn't very well leave for my bed, so I excused myself and went to the men's room. Standing next to me at the urinals was the distinguished-looking, gray-haired gentleman I had first noticed during the Underwear Incident. Both of us said nothing, staring at the white tiles. I flushed, he flushed, and it was after he had dried his hands and discarded the paper towel that he recognized my presence and introduced himself with a little bow: "Stefan von Troubadour." His tobacco-stained fingers dove into his vest pocket and produced a gold-embossed card. I extended a wet hand, but he refrained from taking it and bowed again instead. The card read: Stefan von Troubadour. Senior Partner. Troubadour Troubadour and Troubadour. New York-Paris-London-Donetzk.

"Chet Milosz," I said, "winner of the Nobel Prize in poetry." Not a trace of a smile or chuckle accompanied that statement, I'm happy to report. If the shoes fit, wear them.

He bowed again: "My honor. If you ever need my services...." He spoke as if he had been eating cream-filled chocolate bonbons and was suffering from a sugar overdose.

"Poets rarely have legal problems, but thank you. I'll certainly keep you in mind." I examined the card in order to reinforce the point. I was about to enquire about his specific line of work, when it occurred to me to ask: "Are you legal counsel to—?"

"Herr Doktor Zsasz"—he pronounced it Tsahsts—"and Herr LAY-mon."

"Then they're in excellent hands," I smiled.

"Thank you for your confidence," he smiled back, bowed, clicked his heels, and left.

I examined myself in the mirror. Scruffy, ungroomed, and sickly was the only way to describe my neglected appearance. Two days' worth of facial hair reminded me that, amazingly, I hadn't shaved since Milano. The bloodshot eyes were no surprise, considering how much alcohol I had been consuming. Fortunately, they didn't stand out so much against my sunburnt skin. And the striped red-and-ochre sports shirt actually complemented my face quite nicely. I looked like a surfer dude or ski bum. Were my hair a few inches longer, I might even pass for Adriano Celentano. Too bad I didn't have more chest hair and a raspy voice.

The door swung open and Samuel Livingston Roach walked in. He was visibly surprised to see me; I confess to having been shocked by his size: he couldn't have been more than five feet four.

"Hello," he said coolly, turned on the hot-water faucet, and proceeded to dab at a stain on his tie.

"Cold water works better," I noted with all the gravitas the situation demanded. "Hot water will just reinforce the stain. What is it? Steak juice? Steak sauce? The gravy?"

He spoke with great deliberation and suppressed emotion. "I—don't—know. Poets," he snarled (the word is hackneyed, I know, I know, but there is no other way to capture the totality of conflicted emotions on his contorted face), "should mind their own business. Or—"

"Or else?" I couldn't resist the melodrama, even though I knew full well what he would say.

"Or shut up," he snapped, like a bear trap. (Once again, that overused word—and that unusual simile—best describes his demeanor at that very moment.)

"Sammy, Sammy," I said soothingly, "is this any way to speak to the guest of honor? And a Nobel Prize-winning poet at that?" Proud of my cool, I tapped him on the back, whispered, "See you around, pal" in my best Humphrey Bogart imitation, and made a graceful exit.

Inside the dining room, they were already eating dessert. The waiters were pouring coffee and tea discreetly. The buzzing of the cicadas intermingled with the buzzing of the guests to produce a din akin to a traffic jam. Louise Babylon and Dickey Lemon were laughing. Thor Kriegman was making extravagant gestures and relating something, to the evident delight of his listeners. Jean-Pierre La Baguette appeared to be engaged in a serious conversation with Alla Belomorkanalskaya, although what they had in common I couldn't imagine. Or was the professor flirting? Joe Zsasz stood in a corner, speaking intently into a cell phone. Alexandra Wirrwarr was away from our table, so I took her seat. To my right, the sad-eyed Serge Joupanencoff was pouring himself an exceptionally large brandy and scowling. He had to be the banker. To my left, the equally silent Ariadne Balletmeister—the actress?—was stirring her coffee. With Wirrwarr absent, I attacked the ice cream. "Have mine," my neighbor said. "I can't *stand* gelato." She placed the spoon on the white tablecloth, producing a small brown stain. I've never been able to resist overeating on ice cream, so I grabbed the silver chalice greedily without even pausing to consider the religious symbolism of the act.

"Have you heard about the earthquake?" I asked Balletmeister. It was a transparent ruse to deflect attention from my sacrilegious gluttony.

"You mean the tremors?" (Said with a look of supreme indifference.)

"No, the earthquake, a bona fide *terremoto,* about one hundred miles northeast of here."

"I'm afraid not. Was it serious?"

"Apparently. Several villages were levelled, hundreds were killed. Well, that's what today's papers said."

"Really?" She resumed stirring the coffee. "I would've heard about something that big. You know, you can't believe everything the Italian press says."

"I read it in the *International Herald Tribune.*"

"Really? Isn't the editor an Italian?" The spoon produced another brown stain, a few inches to the right of the first one.

"Well, I suppose you film people don't follow current events too closely."

She looked puzzled, lifted the spoon, and began stirring again. Joupanencoff was busy inhaling his brandy glass, so I nabbed his ice cream. Most of it had melted, so I raised it to my expectant lips, shut my eyes, and enjoyed the velvety liquid slither down my throat. Quite unexpectedly, a once-hazy memory of Saturday afternoons at Vito's luncheonette asserted itself with striking clarity. My father would disappear in the back room, while I sat at the lunch counter with an enormous vanilla milk shake prepared by Vito himself, a bushy-eyed, rotund man who, quite literally, spoke with a soft voice and kept a big stick—I couldn't recall whether it was a blackjack or a baseball bat—beneath the counter. I remembered hoping that Pop's business would last longer than it took to finish the shake. Vito would then say, "Another one, *paisan*?" And I would nod vigorously and plead with him to add just one more scoop, *per favore.* He always did. And then a female voice intruded on my daydreaming.

"Wake up, Mister Milosz, you're dribbling gelato." It was Balletmeister. "By the way, I'm in international finance," she observed. "The drunk to your right is the actor."

"What's your line?" I had a hunch I knew. "Energy, real estate?" I deftly removed the ice cream with a flick of my pinky.

"*Tutto,* as the Italians say." A chuckle—very restrained.

"Mining, shipping?" She said nothing so I took a stab. "Gold and diamonds?"

"*Tutto* means *tutto,* Mister Milosz," she reprimanded me, her eyes as expressionless as grapes. "As a poet, you should know that." A series of chuckles that bordered on tut-tuts.

A persistent tinkle penetrated the din. Joe Zsasz was striking his wine glass with his coffee spoon. "Lay-dees and gennel-mens," he announced. "Good night. Sleep vell. And tomorrow," he paused for dramatic effect, "we vill have great syoor-prize."

My body, and I with it, rose from the table. Balletmeister was stirring her cup again, while Joupanencoff, his head on the table near an overturned brandy glass, was snoring. Across the room, Louise Babylon smiled mysteriously and raised one finger. Was she making a point or signaling one-something? One day? One hour? One what?

I slept that night like the proverbial log. I vaguely recalled dreaming of Ada and Lolita again. It was the oddest thing. They were sitting in plush easy chairs, their legs demurely crossed, and taking turns reciting my poetry (sic!), when a harsh knock on the door disturbed their self-induced reverie. The door flew open, the yellow light streamed in melodramatically, and who but Louise Babylon should creep in like a tigress, disrobe, and engage them in a spirited bout of unusual sexual antics. This was better than a *ménage* with Pnin, but a bit more than my sensitive nature bargained for—even when asleep. I awoke next day feeling even more exhausted than the night before. As I was shaving, I noticed I had a lipstick smudge on my neck. Odd. It had to be Balletmeister: she was the last woman I had seen last night. Doubly odd. I was sure I didn't recall her kissing me good night.

***

The breathless flapping of helicopter blades presaged the arrival of Joe's surprise. I first heard the sound as I was standing at the buffet table, looking out at the lawn, and ladling scrambled eggs onto my plate. I was determined to have a large breakfast that day, lest my hunger lead me to overdose on ice cream again and have sugar-induced dreams that bordered on the all-too-nightmarishly real. The polite cook asked me if I wanted an omelet, but I declined. Three strips of bacon and a heap of hash browns—to be lavishly smothered, in what I knew was an arrogant assertion of America's right to unabashed vulgarity, with ketchup—completed the picture. The whipping sound came nearer and the cypresses and flower bushes began visibly trembling, as if a hurricane were approaching. I joined Dickey, Joe, Serge, and Jean-Pierre just as Dickey had finished saying something about "a good one."

"Heard this in bloody Geneva, chaps. What sound do bloody Italian helicopters make?" A beat went by and no one answered. Dickey began giggling uncontrollably. "Dago"—he placed his hand over his mouth—"dago"—he dropped the hand and tried to assume a straight face—"wop, wop, bloody wop!" "DEE-kee!" Joe cried remonstratively, before throwing back his head and producing a belly laugh. Joupanencoff's face was blank, whether from his hangover or from his lack of comprehension I didn't know. La Baguette wagged his finger disapprovingly and muttered something about negationism. My college would have crucified Dickey for his humor, but this was Europe and we were free of all the New World's quaint antiquarian restraints. I nudged Serge.

"Did you get it?" Dickey's girlish giggling was subsiding.

"*Comment*?" Joupanencoff uttered the word with the verve of a Caligarian somnambulist.

"Why don't you ask them for a shot of something?" Dickey said. "It'll clear the head." Serge moaned in response.

Suspended just above the treetops, the gleaming black helicopter was about to land. Joe and Dickey ran outside to greet their distinguished guests. The rest of us followed and stood in a semi-circle with our backs to the villa. For several seconds, the aircraft fluttered like a huge dragonfly; then it rocked from side to side on the grass and settled down. The women held their skirts protectively. I found myself just behind Thor and Louise. Kriegman stood with his arms folded and a corncob pipe stuck, à la General MacArthur, between his teeth. "Impressive display of power," he said knowingly. La Babylon's arms—I noticed just how hairy they were—were also folded. "Meretricious phallocentrism is all it is. You *would* be impressed, Jake." The propellers came to a halt and five men, all clad in charcoal-gray suits, white shirts, shiny ties, and shiny shoes, disembarked. The largest one—I surmised he was their leader: he wore the only ascot—pumped Joe's and Dickey's hands and then gave each a bear hug and three kisses. He turned to us and waved regally.

"Who is that?" I asked Kriegman. I assumed he had to know.

"The boss man of the U-"—at that moment Thor sneezed—"and one of the richest men in Europe, or so they say. No one really knows how much the guy's worth, but it's either millions or billions. Either way, we're talking really big bucks. Owns half the country, but don't ask me which half. Claims to be building democracy, civil society, blah, blah, and double blah, but is really a tin-pot dictator in charge of a banana republic."

"What's his name?"

"Viktor Illich Zekovich." A chuckle. "They say he chases skirts like the devil himself."

"That lug?" I arched my eyebrows.

"Why are you surprised? Power is an aphrodisiac. In his case, it may be the other way around. Just look at the guy. He's pretty fit for a sixty-something-year old Don Juan in a country where life expectancy for males is about fifty-nine. They say he plays tennis every day, swims the Don in forty-five minutes, and water skis in Yalta. The guy's a bear."

"Looks like a hit man for the Cosa Nostra," I muttered ungraciously.

"You're closer to the truth than you think," Kriegman said. "The fellow spent a few years in jail as a teenager—car theft, rape, maybe breaking and entering. After he got out, he worked his way up the organization: served as an enforcer and shakedown artist. Then, when a rival gang knocked off his boss, he maneuvered a clever power play, took over, and eliminated his rivals. They say he garroted the other gang leader."

"Nice guy. What is he doing here?"

"Look! Joe's handed him a microphone. I wonder what language he'll speak. I don't think he knows English. Oh, my: he's holding the wrong end up!"

"Will you two be quiet?" Louise had poked poor Thor in the ribs. "I can't hear anything with all that yapping."

Zekovich spoke in Russian, methodically, deliberately, monotonously, and almost absent-mindedly, as if he were delivering comments he had memorized and delivered many times before. One of his gray-suited companions, a young man with a high forehead and glasses, translated into passable English. Zekovich said he was honored to be in Caravaggio, at this important—the translator pronounced it "EEM-potent"—gathering of great minds. His country was building demo-CRA-cy and a market E-conomy. The road to both was not straight and narrow, but broad and croo-KED, with many twists and turns that required the wise leadership of a committed leader. (At that point, Zekovich smiled modestly and Dickey exclaimed, "Hear! Hear!") He and his government had made great strides and their people—pronounced "pipple"—supported them and their efforts wholeheartedly and unreservedly. The so-called democratic opposition was corrupt and its leader was a notorious "political whore" (his exact words) who deserved to be where she was—in jail—for crimes against the pipple. Zekovich extended his arms as if to embrace us all. "Come to my cown-tree and breeng your money. Vee velcome eenvestment. I guarantee personally." He devoted several minutes to the "political whore" and I came away with the distinct impression that he had a psychological thing about her. Was he gay? Was the translator's mispronunciation of important a telling Freudian slip? In any case, Joe and Dickey applauded and most of the others joined in with what struck me as unwarranted enthusiasm for boilerplate.

"Ze president has gray-shoos-ly agreed to answer questions," Joe said. "Pleeze, lay-dees and gennel-mens?" A hand shot up. "And pleeze een-troduce you'self."

"Hal Lumumba," a tall, thin, pale man in an aquamarine bow-tie spoke up. "International political advisor with BG and Q. We're based in DC and have contractual relations with scores of emerging democracies. Mister President, your words were inspirational, but I have the following question: How can international investors be sure that their money will be safe? Who can assure them that their investments won't be at risk if the fascist opposition ever comes to power?"

"It's a set-up," I whispered to Kriegman. "Who is this guy?"

"A Beltway bandit, very smart. Used to advise Papa Doc Duvalier and Idi Amin. On their image. Apparently did wonders."

Zekovich grabbed the microphone. "Thank you, Meester Lumumba," his translator said, "you are true friend of my cown-tree and my pipple appreciate your very unconditional support of struggle for better life. You ask: 'How can een-ternational een-vestors know money is in safe hands?' I will tell you how." Zekovich showed the palms of his huge hands to the crowd. "Are my hands being clean? Yes, they are. See? Your een-vestments will be in my hands. And oppo-zee-shoon never come to power. I guarantee it."

Everyone applauded and, once again, Dickey cried, "Hear! Hear!" The next hand went up. It belonged to the stocky little man with golf balls for eyes I had first seen in the parking lot upon arriving at the villa. He had been puffing nervously on a cigarette then and he was puffing nervously on one now. He stepped forward and motioned to us to be quiet.

"Sir, I would like to ask you—"

"Vee all know you are deputy mee-nee-ster of finance, Svven," Joe Zsasz interrupted a tad brusquely, "but pleeze een-troduce you'self."

"My apologies, Joe. Sanjay Palermo, of course—Svven, for short, with two v's. And, as you already know, I'm deputy minister of finance of—"

"The fellow's a big shot," Kriegman whispered directly into my ear. "They say he, and not the PM, makes all the decisions regarding energy and infrastructure. I've heard he gets kickbacks on all the big deals. Sounds quite plausible, if you ask me. Did you notice he hasn't been staying at the villa? Just comes and goes?" I hadn't, but no matter. "He's got a villa of his own across the lake. You'd never guess that his nationality is—"

"Shhh!" It was Louise, of course. "I want to hear this." Her brow furrowed noticeably.

Palermo, meanwhile, had just completed his final sentence, something about wanting to help the president build democracy, and stepped back. A huge smile had spread over Zekovich's face. "Thank you, Meester Palermo, you are true friend of my cowntree and my pipple appreciate your very unconditional support of struggle for building demo-CRA-cy. How to help? you ask. I say: eenvestment, eenvestment, eenvestment! Road to demo-CRA-cy goes through market, as all know."

I quickly glanced at Dickey and, this time, he confounded my expectations by exclaiming: "Bravo! Well done, Mister President! Well done!"

Zekovich then said, "Senk you, senk you, dir friends," placed his wing-like arms around Joe's and Dickey's shoulders, and pressed them tightly to himself. One of the gray-clad men in his entourage snapped a few photos, while Lumumba, Palermo, Balletmeister, Wirrwarr, Belomorkanalskaya, von Troubadour, La Baguette, and a few others approached the trio. Kriegman, Louise, and I withdrew into the villa and poured ourselves some coffee. We sat in a corner of the breakfast room and Kriegman immediately took out his pipe and lit it.

"You don't mind, do you?"

"Filthy thing," Louise said.

"And I love you too," he answered.

"Frankly," I decided to start the conversation, "I'm surprised that La Baguette is so interested in Zekovich. What would a historian of—how did he put it?—history negationism have in common with this lug?"

"My dear Milosz," Kriegman responded, "you're being naïve. Well, I suppose all poets are." His voice trailed off. "No," he adopted the familiar tone of an experienced professor speaking to a doltish student, "you can be certain that your distinguished scholar has a card or two up his sleeve."

"He's just been appointed president of Rogers University," Louise said. "There's probably some fund-raising angle." She smiled mysteriously. "Let me put it another way: you can be certain there's some fund-raising angle."

"It's always about money," Kriegman said matter-of-factly.

"But he's a historian!" I protested. Whence such crashing naïveté I cannot say. Blame it on Bacchus or *bella Italia*.

"Or real estate," Kriegman added, restraining a grin.

"Exactly," Louise continued. "He's replacing some guy who was convicted of taking bribes from local contractors. Jean-Pierre—"

"You know him?" I asked. She smiled; Kriegman winked. In both cases, the adverb slyly applies.

"Jean-Pierre wants to start out with a bang. He's been trawling the world for donors."

"And Zekovich could be one of them?" She smiled again in response, but I persisted. "So what's the quid pro quo?"

"Oh, my dear Milosz! You're embarrassing me. Why respectability, of course! Entrée to all the best circles. Entrée to Europe. Entrée to Ardor Haus. Entrée to the world of higher education. Entrée to the companionship of Nobel Prize winners. Didn't you see how they all adulate him? The man has big clean hands, sure, but what really matters is that he's got big clean dollars and big clean contracts."

"I see," I said morosely. Kriegman was right. I was a naïf. A waif. A babe in the woods. All of this was completely out of my league.

"I bet Zekovich would love to meet you." Kriegman had apparently sensed my mood. "He fancies himself a man of the arts, a philanthropist—a Maecenas, as they say in his part of the world. Hmm, it just occurred to me: that's probably what La Baguette wants from him—a concert hall or, failing that, a basketball arena. Hell, you know better than me how much college sports teams cost."

"I wouldn't know what to say to him." An insincere sigh followed.

"A prize-winning poet at a loss for words!" The sarcasm was Louise's, naturally. "By the way, your jejune glorification of that impossibly phallocentric Rambo was completely gauche—though I must say it went with your outfit." Another mystifying reference to a movie I had never seen! I decided to change the subject.

"So is that why all these people are here? To meet Zekovich?"

"Now your poetic imagination is running away from you, my dear Milosz, and I fear you're engaging in conspiracy theories. No,

Zekovich has a villa not far from here. He was probably vacationing and Joe and Dickey must've figured his presence would add a little spice to our otherwise staid proceedings. Lord knows we could use a bit of pep. Who's in the mood for a snort of scotch? I think I could stand a shot or two right about now. Any volunteers?" He caught a waiter's attention and ordered a round of drinks. "Not to worry: if you can't finish them, I will."

"But here's what I still don't understand," I persisted. "Sure: he wants entrée. I get that. And Jean-Pierre wants a sports stadium. Fair enough. But what do Palermo, Balletmeister, von Troubadour, and all the rest see in him? Why the applause? Why the easy questions? Why the adulation? Your word, Kriegman, not mine."

"Don't be so infuriating," Louise said sharply, "and so naïve. It's money, of course. They all want money. He's got it—loads of it. They want it—as much as they can get their greedy little hands on. Is that so hard to understand? *Tu comprends, mon pauvre idiot*?"

"I'm afraid Louise has hit the nail on the head," Kriegman opined. "There's a lot of *quid* and *quo* sloshing around here. You scratch my back, I scratch yours. Our friends recognized a good opportunity when they saw one. Adulation is a small price to pay for a billion-dollar deal. Or a billion-dollar stadium. You see, my dear Milosz, it's all the same to these people. Art, energy, real estate, you name it—it's all a way of making money. *Das Kapital*, right? Marx would have understood them perfectly."

The door was flung open, a warm breeze ruffled the tablecloths, and Dickey sailed in. "Good news! Good news!" He was positively radiant. "No sessions today! Joe's canceled them. More time for a good chinwag with our guest. Primetime experience, what? Hands on, cutting edge, and all of that. Oh, I bloody almost bloody forgot! Come outside, boys and girls, come outside. Quickly, quickly, everybody. It's about to begin. The president's going to swim across the lake!"

***

Zekovich wore a silver bathing cap and a tiny Speedo swimsuit, black, with two golden lightning bolts embossed on the front and back. His near-nakedness only made him look larger and more imposing, a bit like a Norse god with a penchant for creamy cakes and rich foods. His belly resembled the kind of pointed round shield that Spartan hoplites used to such good effect against the invading Persian armies of Xerxes and Darius. His chest was nothing less than a bear rug. His arms and shoulders resembled legs of lamb. His neck had the thickness of a sirloin steak. Even his buttocks radiated power. There was a mythic quality to his appearance and the only thing that spoiled the *Gesamtkunstwerk*—or total work of art, for those of you with poor educations—was his unusually thin, ostrich-like calves. Zekovich was doing stretching exercises and calisthenics, while his entourage of gray-suited minions stood around him gesturing and talking on their cellphones. Joe was smoking on the dock and appeared to be deep in thought. Dickey was directing the crowd—it seemed like all of us had actually assembled—to come to the water's edge.

"Closer, closer, everybody. Excellent, excellent—quite. Bloody good show about to begin, eh? I say, bloody nice weather, what?" He addressed the translator. "His Excellency all set? Ready to swim the pond? I say! He's in awfully good shape, isn't he?"

By now, Zekovich had also slipped on a pair of cerulean-blue flippers. He waved to us, flip-flapped toward the end of the dock, and jumped into the water feet first. A second later, his head reappeared and he launched into a powerful breaststroke. A minute later, we could barely see him somewhere in the middle of the lake. Then he disappeared. "Heard the one about the Polack who tried to swim the Atlantic?" Dickey began laughing even before delivering the punch line. "He swam half-way, got too tired to continue, and swam back!" Two minutes later, Zekovich's head was visible at the mid-point. I began timing him. It took him exactly seventy-five seconds to grab the edge of the dock with both paws. I had to think of my encounter with Belomorkanalskaya. She was standing on the dock with a white cotton bathrobe draped over her arm. The flippers obviously helped. Still, Zekovich had swum the lake in about four and a half minutes and that was impressive.

He raised himself on his powerful arms and his torso emerged from the water, gleaming like a dolphin. He swung himself around deftly and ended up sitting on the edge of the dock. One flipper came off, then another. Finally, he rose to his feet and handed the bathing cap to one of the gray suits. Another gray suit gave him a towel, which he placed around his neck with a snap. Belomorkanalskaya took a step forward and held out the bathrobe. He had finished inserting one arm into a sleeve when, at precisely that moment, a disobedient gull—was it the same one I had encountered before?—swooped down just above their heads. Frightened, the normally cool Belomorkanalskaya instinctively jerked back, tugged at the robe, and spun Zekovich around. He did an awkward pirouette followed by a jig that was obviously intended to reestablish his balance. To no avail: a second later, he had fallen, head first, into the lake. Belomorkanalskaya produced a fittingly gull-like cry of utter despair. Zekovich's entourage dropped their cell phones; one of them jumped in after their leader. Dickey, whose back had been turned, finally noticed the commotion and shouted, "Someone call 911!" Only Joe Zsasz remained as cool and calm as ever. "Eets only vah-ter." Zekovich emerged a few seconds later, holding his hands above his head like a champion boxer. His wet factotum squished past us on the way to the villa. Order was restored and Joe, laughingly, observed: "Fa-lleenk in vah-ter is like life, lay-dees and gennel-mens. And now—lunch!"

"And after lunch," said Dickey, his composure and dignity fully intact again, "bocce ball!"

***

"Why did you leave me in the grass?" Louise asked as she dropped a breaded veal cutlet onto my plate at the buffet table. "Some gentleman!"

"I'll have another one," I said. "Yes, put it there, right next to the broccoli. And a bit of that ratatouille, if you please. It's right there. See the flowery bowl?" My appetite had become insatiable, quite out of proportion to the eating habits I had at home. "As to the grass incident, well: there was a tremor, as I recall, and lying in the grass was about the safest place to be—which is exactly where you were, as I recall. Unless the earth opened up and swallowed you—which was unlikely—but then it would have been curtains for all of us."

"*Idiot*!"

As an aside, I had to admit that being called an idiot in French was actually quite charming. The English pronunciation is harsh and feels like a swift kick to the butt. Is that because the accent is on the first syllable? Or because the t is hard? The French—ee-dee-O—on the other hand, sounds positively endearing, something that a soft-voiced Frenchwoman might say to her lover on the banks of the Seine or on a moonlit night amid the dunes of Arcachon. Less endearing was the inevitable complement to ee-dee-O: "You can be so infuriating." That, I was beginning to discover, could also be very infuriating. Uncertain about whether I should be attracted to, angry at, disgusted with, or repulsed by Louise—but quite certain that this unexpected march of prepositions pleased me immensely—I joined a table where only one seat was free. She kicked my ankle as she walked by. Either Lumumba or Palermo—I had forgotten which was which—was lecturing to the others: von Troubadour, de Pouff, Roach, Wielkomała, and a swarthy young man I hadn't seen before.

"Come join us, Mister Milosz," von Troubadour said. "We have just been listening to a fascinating disquisition on the nature of democracy. I believe you know everyone, Mister Milosz? Expect perhaps for our belated newcomer—tsk, tsk, my dear boy—Orestes Heldenplatz? Señor Heldenplatz comes to us from Buenos Aires—from the ministry of defense, to be exact. And Mister Milosz—well, he needs no introduction."

As I sat next to the Argentinian, he leaned over to me and said: "Tanks."

Puzzled by his expression of gratitude—was he thanking me for the honor of sitting next to him?—I replied, "You're welcome."

He raised one eyebrow—his left, I think—and tilted his head. "I beg jour pardon, señor?"

"You thanked me," I explained, "and I said you're welcome."

He placed his hands together as if in prayer, brought them up against his nose, and rocked his head from side to side in an apparent display of unrestrained merriment. "Oh, how humorous, how very, very humorous!" His English was formal and he enunciated very clearly and, except for the y's, quite correctly. "I was confiding to jou what my ministerial responsibilities entail and, due to my inadequate knowledge of the great language of Shakespeare, jou presumably imagined that I was one of those exceptionally formal Latin Americans one often finds in the films produced by the Hollywood of yore! Indeed, now that I think of it, *Breakfast at Tiffany's* with the incomparable Miss Hepburn comes to mind. Did jou take me for Holly Golightly's Brazilian paramour, José da Silva Pereira? How humorous, how very, very humorous!" He tittered—literally, if improbably. "Come, Señor Miloss, let us drink to international understanding, outstanding cinema, and the brotherhood of man!"

Our wine glasses clinked and he resumed listening to Lumumba or Palermo about the nature of democracy. I focused on the cutlets, which were a bit greasy, but otherwise delicious. After Lumumba or Palermo finished his disquisition, conversations devolved to pairs. I was the odd man out—for which coincidence I felt eternally grateful to the gods, whether Norse or Greek—and concentrated on the chocolate mousse. Louise Babylon, who deserved to burn in hell, was, no doubt, in seventh heaven. As I wiped my lips and pushed back my chair, I noticed Roach brush his hand against de Pouff's left breast. It was all done very rapidly, as if by accident, with a delicate flick of his wrist while his hand was in mid-air making some point. She inhaled, as if shocked, and said, "Livingston!"—though not reprovingly. I had to smile: I hadn't thought that Fjord's little man had such outsized libertine proclivities. And Madame de Pouff was, evidently, a well-traveled United Nations diplomat who had been around the block more than a few times.

***

There are some sports that I get and some that, try as I might, I do not. I understand and like baseball, American football, and soccer. I understand but don't like basketball and hockey: every minute looks and feels like any other minute and, as far as I'm concerned, both games could be played in exactly one minute. I do not for the life of me get golf. Why grown men and women would whack a little ball repeatedly and follow it up and down artificially constructed landscapes is beyond me. Polo at least has the allure of the chase and, besides, with all those horses and mallets flying around, it's potentially life threatening. But what can happen on the green? An assault by an errant twig, perhaps? A grassy smudge on one's white shoes? The game—golf, I mean—is almost as ridiculous as curling. A well-hit golf ball at least has the merit of producing an impressive whack; brooms on ice can at most go swish-swish.

I provide these brief comments as an introduction to my introduction that day to a game I had only casually observed old Italian men play—bocce ball. They always wore woolen caps, dark vests, and baggy pants and they always waved their arms and swore before and after tosses of the heavy metal balls. These would generally fly in graceful arcs and land in the gravel with barely audible thuds. The point, apparently, was to get one's ball closest to a small ball called a pallina. If an opponent's ball were in the way, the men would throw theirs, more in the manner of softball pitchers, and try to knock the offending ball out of the way. Why the whole thing was called bocce, or who or what bocce was, I had no idea.

In any case, it was soon after lunch and my observation of Samuel Livingston Roach's coy encroachments on the lovely Emilia de Pouff's even lovelier mammary glands that Dickey Lemon announced that the president was hoping to play a good game of bocce with those of us willing to join him. How could I resist the challenge? I had never played the darned thing before, but if ancient Italians in woolen caps, dark vests, and baggy pants could do it, so could I. A group of us led by Dickey and Joe set out for the bocce court. Zekovich and his gray suits were already there. He was wearing a white Polo shirt, white shorts, white sneakers, and knee-length white socks. As at the dock before his swim, he was doing stretching exercises and light calisthenics. Clearly, this was going to be a serious match and I set my jaw in determination accordingly. (That last comment is, naturally, metaphorical, as, in point of fact, my jaw was quite relaxed by the fine meal and the hilarity of my being about to take a whack at something as unlikely-sounding as bocce ball.)

There were seven of us players—Zekovich, Joe Zsasz, Dickey Lemon, Samuel Livingston Roach, Orestes Heldenplatz, Sanjay Palermo, and I. Stefan von Troubadour volunteered to serve as umpire. Each of us was assigned four differently colored metal balls (mine were purple). The grass court was about thirty feet long, which seemed substantially shorter than the courts favored by the old Italians I had observed, but, then again, this was about the only bit of level ground near the villa and we had to make do with what we had. Besides, thirty feet would be less of a strain on our untrained arms. Joe handed the pallina to Zekovich who promptly tossed it into the rose bushes at the far end of the court. One of his gray suits ran after it and quickly emerged, cursing the thorns, with the pallina. I noticed that he had torn his pants. Zekovich lobbed it this time and it settled nicely about twenty-five feet away. The game could begin.

Joe's ball traveled about ten feet and fell with a plop. Roach gritted his teeth and knit his brow—literally and not metaphorically—and, with an underhand motion, overshot the pallina and the court. He struck his hands together in disgust. The visibly inebriated Heldenplatz remarked, "I have seen this played in New Jork," and threw the ball in the manner of a shot putter. It fell some five feet short and he contorted his face in exaggerated disappointment. Dickey and I knocked a few of the other balls, but missed the pallina by several feet. The cool Palermo, a bored expression on his face, perfunctorily tossed the ball and, to everyone's surprise, actually struck the pallina. The ball ricocheted a few inches to the right and all of us cheered.

Zekovich, who, as befit his status, came last, remained impassive. This round was his to win or to lose. He had either to knock Palermo's ball away and hope that his own would come to rest near the pallina or to lob it high above the others and try to make it fall vertically near the target. Zekovich planted his right foot just short of the court and bent over his knee, while making large backwards arcs with his right arm. He had, evidently, decided to go for the lob. Dickey began to say something, but Joe silenced him with a finger to his lips. Remarkably, at least as far as I was concerned, there was tension in the air (not, I hasten to add, literally, but metaphorically, of course). I knew Zekovich wanted to win. I knew he wanted to impress us. Why else had he made a dramatic descent in a helicopter, like some *deus ex machina*? Why else had he swum the lake? Just why he needed to impress people he had never seen before and whom he would, in all likelihood, never see again wasn't clear to me, but there was, I concluded, no figuring these post-Soviet leaders. Was it an inferiority complex? Was it some subliminal awareness of a clash of civilizations? Or did he just like to win at games? I had no clue.

Oblivious of my ruminations, Zekovich straightened his massive body, took two steps backward, while still rotating his right arm, then a quick step forward, and, just as his right foot touched the grass, released the ball. We held our breath. The ball went up, like a high infield pop, and momentarily disappeared in the glare of the sun. Chances were that the ball would land harmlessly on the court. Even so, I decided not to tempt the Fates and covered my head with both hands; the others, evidently inexperienced in the art of playing sandlot hardball, just stood with their faces turned expectantly toward the sky. At that moment, capricious *fortuna* intervened. The ball bounced off Joe's head with a loud crack and struck Zekovich in the nose. Joe crumpled and fell over; Zekovich, stunned but conscious, yelled "*atentat!*" and dove to the grass. In a flash, two gray suits threw themselves on Zekovich, while three gray equivalents produced guns from their underarm holsters, circled their leader, and aimed their weapons at us. The rest of us, terrified and confused, hit the ground as well.

"I say," I heard Dickey's tremulous voice say, "I think there's been a bit of a misunderstanding. Just a ball. Nothing serious. Except—oh, dear—for Joe, whose head looks quite cracked. I say, Mister President, may we get up?"

As one of the gray suits fired a shot into the air (the buzzing of the cicadas ceased immediately) and the others began barking incomprehensibly, the pile of bodies they were protecting suddenly moved (I couldn't help thinking of a *terremoto*) and Zekovich rose, a wan smile offsetting his bloodied proboscis. He brushed off a twig or two from his shorts.

"DEE-kee, my friend!" He gleamed like a new Mercedes. "You

OK? Jov OK?"

"No, Mister President, that's just it. Jov—I bloody mean Joe is decidedly not bloody OK. Will one of you bloody chaps please bloody translate for him? And put those bloody guns away?" Dickey had lost his cool, albeit temporarily. This was a historical moment and I savored it.

Joe groaned. The translator, who apparently also served as Zekovich's first-aid nurse, rushed to the supine Zsasz and examined his head. "Meester Jov ees lahky," he announced matter-of-factly, "for ball not striking heem directly. Veell need few steetches, but should be good as news." He rose to his feet. "Eets life. Acceedents khappen."

An ambulance arrived a minute later and two orderlies whisked Joe away on a stretcher. "I'll be back for bahn-kvet," he declared, a tad too heroically, I thought. "DEE-kee, do not start wee-dout me."

"Sure thing, Joe, ole boy. You'll be fit as a fiddle in no time. What's a bloody banquet without your expert emceeing?"

The ambulance left and the rest of us stood in a circle, uncertain of what to do and increasingly aware of the cicadas that were resuming their clicking with growing force. Tremors were in the air and in the ground and we were at their mercy. The gods were angry with us mortals. Zeus had punished Joe. Who would be next?

"I say," Dickey chirped, "anyone for another round of bloody bocce?"

The others appeared to be nodding their heads in assent, when, mercifully, a huge cumulus cloud suspended directly above us burst and we were drenched within a few seconds. We ran for the house, heads lowered and arms and legs pumping furiously, until we reached the grassy incline and realized we hadn't the strength for that final assault. Except for Zekovich, who ploughed ahead with his wet gray suits in tow. This was not the poor president's day. As he was about to reach the top of the knoll, he slipped and went sprawling into the wet grass. Three of his guards tumbled after him, while the other two stopped in their tracks, horrified, and, in attempting to pull Zekovich to his feet, also fell.

I had had enough and decided not to wait for the denouement. Why not take a swim in the rain? It might be pleasant and, besides, the ritualistic purification appealed to my poetic sensibilities. I ran toward the dock, discarded my clothes, and dove into the water. A second, darker cloud had appeared from nowhere and a lightning bolt flashed and thunder rumbled somewhere in the distance. It all felt very mythic. Here I was, Odysseus, cast into the roiling was were singing, Scylla was to my left, Charybdis to my lops was roaring in pain, while above me the fickle ırreling about my fate. Would I reach Ithaca? Would ...elope still be weaving, unweaving, and waiting? I swam out to the middle of the lake and, with the rain pellets prickling my head, shoulders, and neck, returned leisurely to shore. I donned my pants and returned barefoot to the villa. The young lady at the reception desk observed me crossly as I left mud stains and blades of grass in my wake. A long hot shower followed and I noticed, as I slid under the covers, that I may have strained my right arm. From one measly throw of the bocce ball? I was, evidently, more Ulysses than Odysseus. I expected to take a nap, but fell soundly asleep. Several hours later, as we were assembling for drinks before the banquet, I told Louise about my swim and, like an ill-tempered Medusa, she snapped, "*Idiot*! You could have been electrocuted!"

***

The glossy menu announced that the dishes would be identical to those served at a major-league fête of many years ago:

ARDOR HAUS WELCOMES

THE HONORABLE PRESIDENT VIKTOR I. ZEKOVICH

on the occasion of the anniversary of the
Testimonial Dinner
tendered in honor of
Honorable Maxim K. Litvinoff
Commissar for Foreign Affairs
of the
Union of Soviet Socialist Republics
by the
American-Russian Chamber of Commerce
with the cooperation of
American Russian Institute
Waldorf-Astoria—New York
Friday, November Twenty-fourth
Nineteen hundred thirty-three

Zekovich, obviously, had not just dropped in serendipitously. There had been some serious planning. And if he was being compared to a Soviet commissar, something big had to be in the works. The historical references were too obscure to be the Hamster King's doing, so they had to be the handiwork of Joe Zsasz, who had served, as Dickey put it, in the "NKV-bloody-D" with the "agitprop boys." Joe was playing some kind of historical games. Whatever he was hoping to signal to us great minds, Zekovich would be flattered by the comparison with Litvinoff. Perhaps that's all there was to it? No subtext, just a simple statement of Zekovich's importance to his host? We would, the menu continued, be feasting on:

Beluga Caviar Canapes
Bortschok
Celery Olives
Coulibiac of Lake Trout
Filet de Bouef Strogonoff
New Green Peas Potatoes Noisette
Autumn Salad
Rissolle of Cheese
Bombe Glace Chocolate Praline Wladimire
Gourmandises
Café Filtre

Quite a meal, I thought—although, to tell the truth, I had no idea what most of the stuff was: professorial salaries do not, alas, extend to coulibiacs or pralines Wladimire. But why did Joe and the American-Russian Chamber of Commerce feel that food had to be presented in French? Did Litvonoff speak the tongue? Possibly. Did Zekovich? I'd bet Dickey's life he didn't.

"Do you know what a coulibiac of lake trout is?" I turned to Louise.

"A fish dish," she snapped, yet again, but this time like a ravenous shark.

"It's a kind of pie," Kriegman corrected her. "A Russian staple, I believe."

We were sitting at the same table, together with Joupanencoff, Belomorkanalskaya, and Heldenplatz. Dickey Lemon, Zekovich, and Joe—sporting a square-shaped head bandage and looking exceedingly haggard—were arrayed at the front, a few feet from us and the other three tables. The president's scowling subalterns sat together in visibly wrinkled suits that complemented their dirty collars and stained ties. Zekovich himself was attired in a light blue silk jacket, white slacks, and ostrich-leather shoes. He must have kept the spare clothes in the helicopter.

"I say, may I have your attention?" To my surprise, it was Dickey. "Our fearless leader's had a bit of a knockdown, I'm afraid, and he's asked me—haven't you, Joe?—to take over the helm. Will do, will do—for the good of the cause and all that, I said—didn't I, Joe? Bloody *dreadful* weather we've had today, what? Rained cats and dogs and, I dare say, oxen and sheep." Someone laughed. "But—stiff upper lip, full steam ahead, the show must go on, right? Can't let a little rain stop us, eh? Can't let a bit of mud get in the way of progress, what? So here we are, dry, fit as fiddles—right, Joe?—and ready to charge. The Light Brigade, eh? Over the top! Seize the guns and clean out the trenches! Joe's our general. I'm just the adjutant, but when the going gets tough and all that, eh? The man to my left needs no introduction. Builder, democrat, economist, swimmer, bocce ball player… What else is there to say, eh, Joe? A man of the people, a man of the elites. An indispensable chap and a jolly good fellow, if I may say so myself. A president—may I call you Viktor?—for all times, a leader for all nations. Ladies and gentlemen, may I propose a toast?" Dickey cast his eyes at the menu, where he had apparently scribbled some notes.

"Please raise your glasses and drink to the health of the Honorable Viktor Illich Zekovich, Commissar for Foreign Affairs of the Union of Soviet Socialist Republics!"

"I thought the place had fallen apart," Louise whispered.

"It did," Kriegman responded. "Think of it as poetic license."

"Senk you, senk you, dir friends," Zekovich nodded and downed his bubbly in one motion.

***

The occasion demanded a dramatic interlude—perhaps another cloudburst or, better still, a tremor or two—but we had no such luck. The waiters carried out the dishes and we ate amid the buzz of the conversations inside and the buzzing of the cicadas outside. The bortschok turned out to be good, ole fashioned borscht, not unlike the kind my mother used to make (though hers was incomparably better, of course). The exotically-named coulibiac was just a pastry and fish concoction that went down well with the white wine. The bouef Strogonoff was a bit on the tough side—more Strogonoff, and less boeuf, as Heldenplatz nicely put it—while the new green peas had probably been new before finding repose in some can. The bombe glace satisfied my chocolate craving—though not,

I suspect, Louise's—while the bombastically named praline Wladimire proved to be a pecan praline with a bit of flaccid whipped cream. Not bad, but nothing to write home about. Zekovich was eating and talking and gesturing in Russian. Joe made the pretense of listening, while Dickey stared absentmindedly into space—though, obviously, not into outer space. The minions sat glumly and uncomfortably in their moist suits. Worse, they all appeared to be sipping Pellegrino. The vodka, apparently, was off limits.

"Well," Heldenplatz remarked with affected insouciance, "I do hope we have better weather tomorrow."

"La rain," Joupanencoff muttered. "*Je la* déteste." He appeared to be soused again. "When I am ac-TEEN, la rain ees *absolument terrible*. She fall *et* she fall *et, mon Dieu, c'est impossible*—'ow you say?—to make le film. I get wet, like—'ow you say?—a dahk! Oh là!"

"*Da, da,*" Belomorkanalskaya nodded impatiently. "Have you been to Moscow, Monsieur?"

"Many time!" he boomed. "Oh là là! *J'aime Moscou*! *J'aime la Russie*! *J'aime le peuple russe*! *J'aime Tolstoi*! *J'aime tous le monde russe*!"

"Our friend," Kriegman said dryly, "appears to be a Mother Russia lover. I know the type."

"*Quel type, eh*?" Joupanencoff asked with exaggerated agitation. "*Quel type*? I am *un artiste,* monsieur! I 'ave senseebeeleeTEE! And 'oo are you?"

Thor wisely said nothing for a few seconds and sipped his wine discreetly. He was, I realized, too seasoned a journalist to have responded immediately. He must have known there was no point engaging a drunken Gallic actor in a heated discussion of, well, nothing. Dickey Lemon would probably have said something stupid. Louise would have infuriated Joupanencoff even more. Joe Zsasz might have been able to find the appropriate Delphic utterance to calm his nerves. I was beginning to like Thor "Jake" Kriegman.

"I once saw you in Godard's *Les Trois Mousquetaires,*" Kriegman observed. "I believe you played Aramis, *n'est çe pas*? It was a brilliant performance, on par with that of Jean-Louis Trintignant in *Les Enfants du Paradis*. I congratulate you, monsieur." Was this deliberate mangling of film history a provocation or just sarcasm?

The effect of Kriegman's words on Joupanencoff was immediate. The Frenchman blushed and began stuttering, "*merci beaucoup, monsieur, merci mille fois.*" Then, to everyone's surprise, he withdrew a silk handkerchief from his pocket, blew his nose loudly, and began weeping—not just crying, mind you, not just shedding a tear or two, but positively weeping, though silently and inwardly and not hysterically. Was this a performance? Evidently not. As we watched, unable to do or say anything—after all, what does one say to a weeping French actor: oh là là?—Joupanencoff abruptly pushed away his chair, excused himself, and hurriedly left the table, his head in his hands. Another performance? Whatever the case, he didn't return that evening.

"Well," Heldenplatz said with finality. "I do hope we have better weather tomorrow."

"Should we get another bottle?" Thor asked. I waved to the waiter.

"By the way," Heldenplatz continued, "what is a Mother Russia lover? It is an amusing designation, but I confess to never having encountered it before. Please forgive my ignorance, señor, but the Argentine ministry of defense is not, alas, held in exceptionally high esteem for its cultural endowments. A pity, of course, but that is the nature of the beast and what can jou do?"

"It's someone who barely knows Russia, but immediately goes woozy upon encountering what he believes is the Russian soul," Kriegman pointed out, "which, of course, does not exist."

"I beg jour pardon, señor, but yust what does not exist?"

"The Russian soul." Thor's tone changed, becoming more adamant and insistent. "It's a fiction, a fabrication, a mystification—like every other national soul. Ask Professor Babylon. Isn't that right, my dear Louise?"

"But surely Señor Zekovich has a Russian soul!" Heldenplatz protested. "He swims like a bear and eats like a lion."

"That, my dear Heldenplatz, just makes him Russian."

Like a sleepy hyena, Louise expelled a loud yawn. "Can we talk about something else, boys? I'm bored."

Notwithstanding her bluntness, I thanked the heavens for her interruption: I, too, was experiencing the relentless onslaught of creeping ennui. I glanced at the other tables. Zekovich, Joe, Dickey, and the companions had vanished. The other participants were still in their seats, having quarter-hearted conversations and picking at what remained of the cheeses. Roach was seated next to de Pouff again, with their backs to me, and his left arm was caressing her bare spine (nicely curved, as in that swell painting by Ingres). La Baguette and Lumumba were arm wrestling. Von Troubadour had lit a thick Cuban cigar and was blowing blue smoke rings at the ceiling. Belomorkanalskaya had ordered grappa; she contorted her face like a turtle every time she took a sip. It was hard to believe that the second day of our gathering was coming to an end.

"You can be so infuriating," Louise said with a voice like ice. "I'm bored. Amuse me."

"Would you like me to recite one of my poems?"

"In Polish?" Her eyes grew the size of clams.

"Of course." I actually knew a line from Adam Mickiewicz. I had no idea how to pronounce it, but she'd never know the difference: *"Litwo! Ojczyzno—"*

"Funny language. LEET-woah-oy-ZIZ-no: sounds Yiddish. Was this Mikevych guy Jewish? Never heard of him. Anyway, what did you just say?"

"The music of the words conveys the meaning. You should know that. Now listen again. I'm experimenting with Latin haikus." I was about to recite the first line of Vergil's *Aeneid* (who doesn't know that stirring example of dactylic hexameter—*Arma virumque cano, Troiae qui primus ab oris*?), when, like a somnolent lioness who'd just dined on a plump antelope, Louise yawned ostentatiously.

"Great stuff, Chester—*really* great stuff. Like all your stuff." She blew us all loud kisses. "Good night." We watched her waltz out of the room.

The others hadn't been listening anyway, so I scraped the bottom of my dessert cup, drank the bit of warm wine in my glass, and followed her upstairs. But not, as you might be thinking, into her room. That would've been *idiotique*. Instead, I broke out in uncontrolled giggles on the staircase. I had just remembered that a paleontologist colleague had once asked me whether dactylic hexameter was a dinosaur. The girl at the reception desk glared at me disapprovingly and pressed a long finger to her stern lips.

FOUR

C. Milosz rows in tune to Wagner's Valkyries, solves the mystery of the Underwear Incident, and gets some Grey Poupon in his ear

I slept badly. Was it the coulibiac or was it the beluga caviar? Beside the proverbial tossing and turning, there was also an endless, and endlessly tiring and tiresome, dream, sparked no doubt by my experience at dinner of Aeneas *interruptus*. Troy was burning, the Greeks were massacring the city's inhabitants, and the gods were displeased, but several of us still managed to escape. For some reason, I was carrying Joe on my back, while Dickey was, of all things, Laocoön, going on and on about how he had known from the start that the Horse was a ruse, that we should've listened to him, and that he had told us so. And where were you when Cassandra was center-stage? I asked as we boarded a ship. The dream then shifted to North Africa and Dido, who appeared in the guise of the lovely Emilia de Pouff. This part should've been enjoyable—after all, Aeneas gets the girl—but it turned nightmarish, perhaps because I had witnessed her incomprehensible responsiveness to Roach's amorous advances. As I watched her commit suicide—in Vergil's version, I'm long gone—I remember thinking, maliciously, that her departure couldn't have come a moment too soon. We boarded the ship and Joe intoned, "I fear the Greeks, even when they bear gifts," to which Dickey replied: "A whisper in the howl of history!" And off we set for Italy, but not before a gaggle of Cyclopses swam alongside the ship like frolicking dolphins and Scylla and Charybdis performed a rousing rendition of "*Quando, Quando, Quando*." It was a mess. Fortunately, we reached Latium and some huge hound directed me to the Underworld, which turned out to be a neon-lit version of Dante's Inferno, where, perhaps unsurprisingly, I came upon the participants of our gathering engaging little satanic creatures in conversation. Zekovich and Döner Kabob were doing backstrokes in the molten lava and calling on me to join them.

It was just as I was about to throw caution to the wind and dive in that I awoke, feeling exhausted, singed, and terribly thirsty. I shook my head like a mutt shaking off water. Where were Ada, Lolita, Anna, and, even, the miserable Pnin when you needed them?

Had they abandoned me? Were they stand-ins for the Muses? If so, I groaned, I was in serious trouble. Their fleeting appearance a day or two ago could be interpreted as boding the end of my writer's block. Their conspicuous absence from my nocturnal peregrinations couldn't be a hopeful sign, especially as they should've felt quite at home in such a classical setting. Or were they pleased by my forays into Vergil and too embarrassed to admit it? In that case, the dream and their absence was actually a good omen. The evidence pointed to both interpretations and, frustrated as always by what my colleagues in the philosophy department call the underdetermination of reality, I resolved to listen to my gut, which, usually, serves as a good guide. This time, however, all my gut told me was that I was famished. Not once during my dream had we eaten and, although Dido had offered her ample fruits (I no longer remembered whether she was being serious or whether that was just a metaphor for oh là là), I had declined—stupidly, I now realized.

Why go hungry, even in a dream? I glanced at my watch. It was six-thirty and the breakfast buffet would already be laid out. I could grab a coffee and a few croissants and, with a little luck, return to my room without encountering anyone. Aeneas wouldn't have slunk along a staircase with pockets full of Latin pastries, but the dream was over and I felt no obligation to continue living life according to his impossibly high standards. Besides, he had not yet founded Rome in my dream, so that, as far as I was concerned, he was just a Trojan on the lam. The croissants, I'm happy to report, were excellent. I placed six in my shaving kit and, like a fugitive acolyte of good King Priam, ran back to my room and ate them at the window. The sky was a solid blue again. The mountains in the east glowed like heaps of candy. A breeze blew and the tops of the cypresses, like feathers, shook almost imperceptibly. Did I have the strength to endure a third day of the seminar? I collected the crumbs, threw them out the window, observed several sparrows descend on them like hawks, and stepped into the shower. No, I did not.

***

Tedium can be quite tedious and, instead of attending the day's proceedings, I decided to play hooky and seek refuge in—where else?—the middle of the lake. Getting to the dock would require some finessing, however. If I took the main stairs, I was sure to run into Joe or Dickey or the others and would have to join them in the conference room. Louise would likely corral me and then I'd be a dead duck for the rest of the day. But I reckoned that old Italian villas had to be crawling with servants' staircases. Mine was at the end of the gilded corridor, where the red carpet was especially frayed and thin. One door led to a linen closet. The other opened on a narrow, ill-lit concrete stairwell that had been painted a uniform industrial gray. Clouds of cigarette smoke rose from the floor below: this was, I surmised, probably where the villa's personnel took their smoke breaks.

Twenty steps later, I reached the ground-floor landing, but, instead of encountering waiters, I came upon none other than Zekovich and two of his gray-suited minions. They stood silently, their right knees extended and their right feet propped against the wall, looking like the bored understudies of a male chorus line. I excused myself and wished them a good morning, but they said nothing, their eyes half-closed, their nostrils slightly flared. The two gray suits were about Zekovich's height and, if it weren't for his noticeably more elegant attire, I wouldn't have known who the president was and who the body guards were. Our school president or Kabob would, I suspected, have been equally at a loss. She hobnobbed with the rich and powerful on her fundraising expeditions to the Hamptons and South Beach, while Kabob exploited his Turkish roots in his search for millionaires with elegant homes on the Bosporus. I doubted that their marks smoked cigarettes in stairwells with the hired help. Well, at least Zekovich favored Western tobacco, and not the vile variety preferred by most of Big Mama Russia's filthy children. "See you later," I said with as much devil-may-care casualness as I could muster, pushed against the iron door, and, after enduring an extended creak, was immediately blinded by the glare outside. As the door closed behind me, I distinctly heard an outburst of guffaws from within. I wish I had thought of Plato's parable of the cave, but, alas, I did not.

I figured I'd avoid the main path leading directly to the dock and, instead, veer off to the left, cross the lawns with the poinsettias, guava plants, and rose bushes, disappear behind the palm grove located on the slope of the hill that formed the greater part of the promontory, cut back to the right, head for the shore, and then work my way along the brush toward the inlet and the dock. It was a roundabout way of going some two hundred feet, but I'd be highly unlikely to encounter anyone in the bushes at this time of day. Besides, Aeneas could do no less.

It should go without saying that I miscalculated the ease of traversing the wooded area beyond the perfect plastic lawns. The terrain was rocky and my sandals kept slipping on the moss. The slopes leading down to the lake were overgrown with some thorny undergrowth and at one point I even stepped into a colony of red ants. I came upon the remnants of a barbed-wire fence and had to negotiate the tangles with my bare and exceedingly vulnerable legs. Were there snakes and iguanas? Probably not, but then again, how could I be sure? And what of ticks and other deadly insects, lizards, and vermin? The fall of Troy looked easy compared to my travails (a silly comparison, I admit, but I was hot and tired, so please show some forbearance and look the other way).

Two hours later, I emerged from the bushes and stood on a cliff, some twenty feet above and to the left of the dock. Twenty feet may not seem like much (why, it's the length of most studio apartments in Manhattan!), but it is if one has to negotiate a straight vertical drop with few toeholds. One hour later, I stood on the dock, looked up at the villa, which appeared to be palpably near, and wondered how I could have spent the entire morning on so short a distance. A fresh breeze blew in from the lake and, exhausted by my trek, I crawled into the rowboat and shoved away. If Belomorkanalskaya was in the water, I'd just keep rowing. In the state of nature, it's every man for himself. This time, I was determined to enjoy the peaceful lapping of the water with only my thoughts as companions.

I had reached the mid-point of the lake, roughly the spot where Zekovich's head had become too small to see. The villa was fully visible at the top of the hill. The seminar participants were milling about on the lawn; an outdoor lunch buffet was evidently in the works. Zekovich's massive frame was easy to spot. Standing next to him were, apparently, Joe and Dickey and some of the suits. I could see two figures dash behind the palm grove to the right. Were they Roach and La Pouff? Probably. Louise was in red again and her torpedo bra couldn't be missed. The man she was talking to was probably Thor Kriegman. Like flies, two waiters flitted from person to person pouring wine. Another two carried hors d'oeuvres on silver trays that shone intermittently like an infernal Morse code device. I was hungry and thirsty and my stomach produced unseemly noises, but I focused on the rowing, the playfulness of the waves, and the cool breeze and soon was deep in thought.

This whole conference was quite obviously a show, a scam of some kind. Even a naïf like me could see that. Joe Zsasz and Dickey Lemon were the masterminds, so much was clear. Zekovich was also part of the plan, though just what the plan was and whether there was in fact a concrete plan I didn't know. Most of the other guests appeared to have been invited to further Joe and Dickey's ends. Was anyone on the level? Was anyone a great mind? Well, I was. *Cogito, ergo sum,* I thought. Who else? Serge Joupanencoff was probably who he said he was: a mediocre French actor who drank too much, didn't know French cinema, and suffered from bouts of self-doubt. I couldn't imagine his being anything but the perpetually soused and morose image he projected. Louise Babylon might be for real as well. A feminist who specialized in—what was it exactly?—civil society and globalization or some such thing couldn't have been made up. As someone without a sensible excuse for existing, she seemed much too useless to be of any use to Joe and Dickey. Thor Kriegman? Jean-Pierre La Baguette? I was leaning to fifty-fifty odds with them. The others had to be in on whatever Joe and Dickey were concocting.

And what exactly was that? I had no idea (*obviously,* you will snort with, alas, complete justification). It was certainly underhanded and it was definitely financial, but, since those two adjectives applied to the vast majority of human undertakings, it did me little good to know that their scheme was, well, a human undertaking. Big finance (Balletmeister, Roach, and Palermo), big real estate (Belomorkanalskaya), big energy (Palermo), big technology (Wielkomała), big weapons (Heldenplatz), big law (von Troubadour), and big politics (Wirrwarr, Lumumba) were all represented and Zekovich appeared to have a finger or toe in all the pots. Some kind of negotiation was taking place and some kind of deal was in the works. And whatever it was, Joe Zsasz the ex-communist-turned-Svengali and Dickey Lemon the Hamster King-turned-Maecenas were at the center of the action.

So why were Joupanencoff and I and maybe Louise and Thor here? As window dressing? As diversions? As the pretty faces adorning whatever reports and brochures would eventually appear? I had to remind myself that, strictly speaking, it wasn't I who was here: it was my near-namesake, Chess-wow. I supposed they had reckoned that, with a bona fide Nobel Prize winner in tow, the enterprise would look legitimate to whoever chose to apply a magnifying glass to the proceedings—and procedures. Perhaps Chess-wow was the linchpin of the whole operation? The theory was attractive, in a lurid sort of way, but I had to dismiss it upon closer consideration. If Chess-wow was the key, they would've tried to implicate me in their planning to a far greater degree. Instead, it was striking how little attention anyone paid to me. They greeted me, made a remark or two about my poetry, and then moved on. And they never seemed to be disturbed by my unexplained absences. No, whether Chess-wow or me, we were both window dressing. Did Joe know Chess-wow from way back when? No, that couldn't be, as he would have immediately recognized me as an imposter. They had wanted Chess-wow precisely because he was Chess-wow. They specifically wanted a Nobel Prize winner, because having a Nobel Prize winner in their midst made them feel good about themselves and the circles within which they consorted. The world's highest form of creative recognition was, for them, the equivalent of a shiny trinket, a fast car, or a lobster dinner. I was here because they thought I was Chess-wow and Chess-wow had been invited because they liked his bling. It was that simple.

On the other hand, the digs were good, the food was fine, and the setting was magnificent. I had met some interesting people—or was it more accurate to call them interesting types?—I had learned a few things about the ways of the world beyond my campus and the ivory towers on which it rested, and I had had several interesting experiences. There was nothing to kvetch about, except of course that the whole thing was an outlandish con game of some kind. Well, I had never met a grifter and I had never been part of a swindle and there was, as they say, always a first time for everything. On second thought, that last statement wasn't quite true. Our esteemed president was a grifter and Kabob was a con man and one wouldn't be completely off target in believing that the manner in which the EDI—that's the Excellence Diversity Index, in case you've forgotten, which measures the ratio of the ratio of excellence to diversity to the ratio of diversity to excellence—is compiled was a swindle. It was reassuring to know that Joe and Dickey's inner circle appeared to consist of no academics and that Louise Babylon and I were here only for show. Whatever one might intimate about the dishonesty that dripped from the trees in the grove of academe, there was much more of the gooey stuff to be found in other branches of life.

If I were a prose writer, the last few days would've provided enough inspiration and material for a lifetime of savage scribbling. But I was not. I was a poet and I was a poet who hadn't written any poetry in years. Filth, decay, degeneracy, and decrepitude might have inspired Charles Baudelaire. My sensibility was more of a Frostian or Dickensian nature. Trees and fences and other mundane objects turned me on, as did fleeting glimpses. Of what? You might ask. The truth? Of anything. It could be some Big Insight into the nature of reality. More often than not, it was just a glimpse of something beautiful, something out of the ordinary—such as the orange trolleys sailing along the shadows of Milano's tree-lined boulevards that almost inspired me to write a poem—or something exceedingly ordinary, such as a crooked finger or an empty coffee cup's relation to an ashtray. The people I had met, the conversations I had had, and the experiences I had undergone had not thus far set my Muses in motion. If anything, I feared they had dulled them into an even deeper slumber.

But perhaps a little abuse is just what the doctor ordered for the Muses? Perhaps they needed to be jostled, not mollycoddled, commanded, not implored? Perhaps a swift quick in their flabby butts is just what my stay at Ardor Haus was in the process of producing? Perhaps they'd be awakened from their lethargy and, like enraged Valkyries, storm to my side? What did they sing as they did their Wagnerian ride? Hoja Ho O! Hoja Ho O! Hoja Ho O! I quickened my rowing pace—pulling hard on Hoja and letting the rowboat ply ahead on Ho O. Odysseus, Aeneas, Dido, the Valkyries: the exhilaration was overpowering and I rowed and rowed ceaselessly, carelessly, crisscrossing the lake in zigs and zags, and breathing in the fresh air as if it were perfume. After an hour or two or more, I placed the oars in the boat and sat still. My mind was empty (or, if you like, even emptier than it usually is). The sun warmed me, the water and wind cooled me, and I dosed off again.

Did I dream again? I recall only disjointed images: Zekovich in the lava, Louise in the grass, Dido on a pyre, Joe Zsasz haranguing a group of workers, Dickey assaulted by hordes of lemmings and hamsters. Perhaps I would've remembered more had it not been for the mighty crack that suddenly assaulted my ears and my subsequent unexpected immersion in the cold lake. At first panic-stricken—is this how I would meet my end?—I gulped like a fish, drank in some oily water, and flailed about like a windmill with my arms and legs. After a few seconds, I regained my composure and sense of presence. I was afloat. I would not, like the villa's former owner, come to rest in a watery grave. The rowboat had been rammed and smashed by a yacht or ferry. I looked up at the curious heads bobbing above the railing like pigeons on a clothesline and the fingers and hands fluttering toward me. There, unmistakably silhouetted against the pulsating ultramarine sky, were Joe Zsasz and Dickey Lemon! A rope ladder uncoiled like a pair of snakes. I grabbed it and, after some maneuvering, managed to place my hands and feet on the rungs and, swaying and shaking, pull myself upward. Near the top two hairy arms grabbed me. I slid over the railing and landed on my back. The same hairy arms took hold of my shoulders and set me upright.

"*Tovarishch!*" It was the burly Russian Alberto and I had met in the Bar-Ristorante Benito. He yanked me to my feet and enveloped me in a bear hug. "*Tovarishch!* Ree-MEM-ber? Boom-boom, yes? Bar, yes?" I nodded weakly. "*Tovarishch!*" He gave me a slap across my back and I lurched forward. "Zhenya, Vanya, Tolya," he called and the three other elephantine Russians in blue Adidas tracksuits appeared and grinned their creamy grins at me.

"I say, my dear chap," Dickey intervened, "no introductions necessary, eh? Ole pals, you and the president's body guards, what? A reunion, eh? Bloody wet, though. Odd place to be taking a nap, what? In the middle of the bloody lake? Could've been a bloody mess. A bloody nigger in a bloody woodpile. A bit of a swim, eh? Bloody nice weather, though, bloody nice bloody weather. Follow me, ole boy. Down below—dry clothes. About the same size as me, what? Look like twins, look like bloody twins!"

***

I emerged from the hold wearing Dickey's khaki shorts and pink Polo shirt, but not before making a major discovery. Unexpectedly, Dickey had also thrown me a pair of underwear. As it turned out, they were identical—Ralph Lauren jockey shorts—to the soiled pair I had encountered a few days before in the Underwear Incident. Just how the suave Dickey Lemon's soiled shorts found their way to a pile of luggage in the parking lot at the villa I did not know and was unlikely ever to discover. (I confess that my accumulating ignorance, as expressed in serial I-did-not-knows, was beginning to infuriate, flummox, and discombobulate me.) Did the Hamster King place them in his pocket and then, after wiping his sweaty brow, drop them in panic—or disgust? Or did the shorts just fall out of his suitcase? But how likely was it that cool Dickey Lemon was such a dismal suitcase packer? Or was someone trying to set him up? And who would be so refined as to utilize dirty underwear? I recalled that the East German secret police, the Stasi, collected dissident underwear in special jars, just in case they needed to track down regime opponents with dogs. And wasn't Joe Zsasz the only person at the meeting with some connection to the communist secret services? Had Joe turned against Dickey? Had Dickey turned against Joe and was getting his comeuppance? There were too many questions. Where was Mister Moto when I needed him? Well, I thought as I slipped on the Ralph Laurens and admired their slim fit, at least the mystery of the Underwear Incident had been solved.

As soon as I stepped out onto the deck, however, I was greeted with another mystery. I hadn't paid much attention to the people on the yacht in my hurry to change my clothes, but, now that I was dry and was cradling an oversized cognac in my hand, I realized they were no strangers. There were of course the four large Russians in jogging outfits. More striking was that the entire Ardor Haus crowd appeared to have been transplanted to the boat: Wirrwarr, Joupanencoff, von Troubadour, Belomorkanalskaya, Palermo, Heldenplatz, Roach, La Baguette, de Pouff, and all the others. Joupanencoff, whom I had taken for a hopeless lush, was a surprise, but even more of a shocker was the presence in the bow—or was it the stern?—of Louise Babylon and Thor Kriegman. Joe Zsasz must have noticed the befuddled look on my face.

"You ver avay, Chess-wow," he poured me more cognac and puffed on his cigar, "and vee moved conference here. CEE-gar? DEE-kee, please geeve Chess-wow a CEE-gar." Joe was wearing a sailor's hat, presumably to hide the bandage on his head.

"I was the whisper in the howl of history?"

"I say," Dickey laughed, "that's my bloody line! Bloody good, though—bloody, bloody good! Bravo, bravissimo, and all that. By the way, fancy a cigar, ole boy? Cuban. Smooth as silk, eh? Cohibas, Montecristos, Partagas—have them all."

"No, thank you."

"You sure, ole boy? Illegal across the pond, you know? Throw you in a bloody dungeon, tear out your fingernails, beat the soles of your dainty feet. The CIA or FBI or IRS or whatever you Yanks call them."

"Just a bit more cognac, Joe," I said, noticing that I had downed the entire glass in a few seconds. My nerves had steadied and, despite the creeping warmth in my shoulders and neck, I finally felt level-headed and focused. It was only then that I came to apprehend what I had been looking at but not seeing. Except for Joe, Dickey, and the four Russians, all the men were wearing skimpy bathing suits that barely contained their buttocks. Most of the women were topless. Both sexes—I refuse to say genders: sorry—were holding drinks and laughing and smoking. I must have looked surprised again and Joe said, as he filled my glass, "Zis is EE-taly, Chess-wow. Zere is no poo-ree-ta-NIZM here."

"I say, ole boy, no need to go gaga over a few titties," Dickey remarked. "God's handiwork, Nature's provenance, and all that, what? Body needs to breath. Beautiful weather, eh? Skin is an organ, you know that? Bloody right it is. Organs need air, eh? No bloody whisper in the bloody howl of bloody history, eh? I say, you sure about the cigars? Cohibas bloody splendid. Blue bloody sky, bloody cognac, bloody Cohibas, bloody titties! Top of the world, eh? Not a single bloody nigger in the woodpile, what?"

"So what's today's agenda?" There obviously wasn't any.

"REE-lahk-say-shun," Joe said.

"Need to take a break, what? Ole brain cells can't go clickety-clack, clickety-clack all the time." Dickey began making an oval motion with his right hand. "Clickety-clack, clickety-clack, clickety-clack! Always loved trains. Even as a boy. Clickety-clack, clickety-clack, clickety-clack! Woo-woo!"

"Vot is voo-voo, DEE-kee?"

"Sound a train makes, Joe. Didn't know? Boy's best friend, a choo-choo. Not a bloody dog. Too bloody bothersome. Needs to be fed. Needs to be walked. Needs to be bathed. Slobbers all over you with his tongue. Bloody hell, what? Right, Chester? Bloody right I'm right! Nothing like a train for a young boy, eh? Nothing like a bloody choo-choo train."

"I suppose you're right, Dickey." The cognac had gone to my head and I was willing to agree with anything he said. "My father used to ride the—" Dickey's cell phone rang before I could finish the sentence.

"Got to run, ole boy! So sorry! The president needs me." And off he ran, followed by Joe. I finished my cognac and, bumping and brushing against gaggles of beer bellies, hairy chests, bursting buttocks, and bouncing breasts, made my way as quickly as I could in my quasi-inebriated condition to the bikini-clad Thor and the bare-chested Louise. At the sight of so much pulsating cellulite, I should have been either repulsed or excited. Instead, my poetic side got the upper hand and I saw in my mind's eye Bill Haley and his inimitable Comets swing their guitars and sing: "We're gonna rock around the clock tonight. We're gonna rock, rock, rock 'til broad daylight. We're gonna rock, we're gonna rock, we're gonna rock around the clock tonight."

I'll be the first to admit that Bill's lyrics aren't great poetry; they may not even be poetry—though they're certainly no less poetic than much of what passes for poetry nowadays. But you've got to admire the alliteration, the repetition (or anaphora, as we poets call it), and the rhythm: the drive, the spirit of the thing. And then it struck me: Wasn't Bill just following in Edgar Allen Poe's venerable footsteps? Wasn't Bill just "Keeping time, time, time, in a sort of Runic rhyme, to the tintinnabulation that so musically wells from the bells, bells, bells, bells, bells, bells, bells—from the jingling and the tinkling of the bells"? This unexpected encounter with bare-faced intertextuality sent shivers—literally—down my spine. I was, I knew, in the presence of inspiration and, through it, in the presence of Art. My Muses were knocking! My Muses were on board with me! They would find me as surely as I would find them! (Pardon the three consecutive exclamation points, but my excitement was irrepressible. So here's a fourth!) I knocked back the remaining cognac and asked a passing waiter to refill my glass.

Thor and Louise were leaning over the railing and had their backs to me. Please believe me when I say I've been in the presence of aesthetically more satisfying—or, if you like, less disturbing—sights. Details are surely unnecessary: the backs and buttocks of journalists and professors have, I believe, rarely served as the subjects of a painter's gaze. As to me, suffice to say that I instinctively jerked my head to the right and closed my eyes. However involuntary the motion, it proved to be a strategic mistake. I lost my balance and, hands and arms outstretched like a skydiver's, went flying in the direction of the buffet table. The canapés made for a soft landing, but my head struck something hard and—the cliché is quite appropriate in this instance—I was out like a light. The last thing I remember seeing was a large jar of Grey Poupon mustard.

***

It was the pungent smell of mustard that awoke me. Ada, Lolita, Anna, Dido, and I had been frolicking on some nudist beach in North Africa—how I could tell I don't know, but I knew that's where we were—when the girls suddenly groaned and said they were famished. Anna had prepared some blinis and Dido had brought some couscous; we devoured everything in a flash, drinking it down with Lolita's soda pop. "And now for some hotdogs!" Ada exclaimed. "A capital idea!" I said, using a modifier-noun combination I had never before used in all my life. Suddenly, we were fully clothed and walking along a boardwalk, eating cotton candy, popcorn, and ice cream. Zekovich was with us, wearing a floppy straw hat, Bermuda shorts, and flip-flop sandals and biting into a candied apple. "A khotdog stand!" Anna cried in her all-too-Russian accent. And then, just as suddenly, we were all munching on juicy frankfurters with sauerkraut, mustard, ketchup, and relish. "Umm," Zekovich said, "better than caviar!" "Umm," Dido said, "I must bring this to my people." "I've had better," Lolita yawned, visibly bored, and threw her dog away. The rest of my dream was a blur. The hotdog hit the ground at just the moment that Anna took a step forward and a kiddie choo-choo train appeared. With my extensive literary background—for some reason I was carrying a copy of Tolstoy's collected works with me—I knew that this conjunction of coincidences could only mean one thing: Anna would fall under the train! Life, I instantly decided, could not imitate art! I lurched forward and grabbed her by the collar. She squealed like a hamster, but the train chugged past us and she was saved. However, in my excitement, I had inadvertently squeezed the bun and squirted the mustard into my face: unlike the others, I had ordered my hotdog without the works. I sniffed the air. Had I only dreamed of mustard or were residues of the stuff still in my hair?

Like the hero of some pulp-fiction detective story, I was lying on a narrow bed in a dimly lit stateroom with a slow-moving ceiling fan. The only thing missing was the faint smell of gunpowder. I found the bathroom, clicked on the light, and examined myself in the mirror. The canapés had left only a few traces on my shirt. There appeared to be some encrusted mustard near my nostrils. Well, that accounted for the smell. I scrubbed my face with cold water and soap, ran wet fingers through my tousled hair, and decided I looked presentable enough to return to the festivities. The others would laugh, as well they should. I would also laugh and be a good sport. Of course, there was also the possibility that they were all so besotted by now that they would have forgotten what transpired. I looked at my watch. It was four o'clock in the afternoon. I had slept for several hours. If the party were still going strong, there was no need to fear any ridicule.

I climbed the narrow squeaking staircase to the deck, expecting to hear raucous laughter and the buzz of conversation. But, except for one voice—it was unmistakably Dickey's—it was quite quiet. As I stepped into the main room, one of the Russians in the tracksuits took my elbow and guided me solemnly to a seat in the back. Assembled before me was the entire group, attired in their regular day clothes. At the front was a table, behind which sat Joe, Dickey, and Zekovich. Stacked before them were three piles of documents and Zekovich was busy signing them and passing them on to Dickey and Joe for their signatures.

"What's going on?" I whispered to Alexandra Wirrwarr, who was sitting next to me.

"Contracts."

"Contracts? What kind of contracts? For books?"

"Of course not," she said impatiently.

"Then for what?"

"Deals."

"Deals? What kind of deals?"

"Big deals."

"What kind of big deals?" I was getting exasperated.

"Very big deals."

"Big money?"

"Is there any other kind?" she said and ostentatiously turned her head away.

Very well, it was perfectly, painfully obvious that some serious deal making was taking place. It was just as obvious that Zekovich, Dickey, and Joe were the principals and that all the others were somehow involved. I recalled my earlier ruminations. Here were representatives of big finance, big real estate, big energy, big technology, big weapons, big law, and big politics. The bigs of the world had decided to unite, knowing they had nothing to lose but their small change. (That wordplay on Marx's famous rallying cry actually occurred to me on board, at that very moment, I'm proud to report.) If Wirrwarr was mum, so too would the others be. I could only surmise that the assembled bigs were all signing very big deals with Zekovich and that Joe and Dickey were serving as middlemen. It was also obvious that the boat had departed without me intentionally. I was the odd man out. But it was no less obvious that, contrary to my earlier calculations, Serge Joupanencoff, Louise Babylon, Pierre La Baguette, and Thor Kriegman were involved in this thing as much as the others. Just what a bad actor, a bipolar scholar, a self-obsessed historian, and a washed-up journalist could offer Zekovich or, for that matter, Joe and Dickey was beyond me. And Joe and Dickey's decision to exclude me from their schemes both flattered and annoyed me. Was I too important or too unimportant to be involved? I didn't have time to pursue this line of thought, however, as Wirrwarr leaned toward me, apparently ready to share some confidence.

"Forgive me for saying so, Mister Milosz," she observed, "but you appear to have mustard in your ear."

"In my ear?"

"That's exactly what I said."

I was fumbling for a more coherent repartee, perhaps even an off-the-cuff joke, when, fortunately, a *deus ex machina* in the form of Joe Zsasz intervened. "Lay-dees and gennel-mens," he announced, "our vork eez done. Bravo, Meester Prezeedent! Bravo, DEE-kee! Bravi to all you!" With each sentence, his right hand punctuated the air with the glowing cigar. A nice touch, I thought, reminiscent of Fidel. A huge smile worthy of the exaggerated idiom, from ear to ear, was glued to his face. His eyes glowed like diamonds. The pipple applauded. Dickey rose from his chair and, after clearing his throat loudly, placed both forefingers to his lips. Like a gunshot, the applause ceased immediately.

"Good show all around," he said, his silver hair radiating enthusiasm, "good show all around. Heaps of gratitude to this man"—and he looked benevolently at Joe—"for being the brains. His idea, his genius, his initiative—his bloody show! Wouldn't be here without him. Would probably be in some pub, eh? Drowning my sorrows, eh?" He laughed and was greeted with a round of titters. "Heaps of gratitude to you, ole boy! Heaps of gratitude for bringing us here. Heaps for being a bloody genius. Heaps for bringing a bit of filthy lucre into our sad lives, what?" Dickey clapped Joe on the back and the others applauded. "I say, ladies and gentlemen, mustn't forget one more chap, eh? Mustn't forget the fellow who took our extended hand. Mustn't forget a great humanitarian, a visionary leader—President Viktor Ze-KO-vich!"

And then, to my surprise, Dickey launched into "For He's a Jolly Good Fellow" and was joined, as if on cue, by the entire assembled audience. When they finished, Wielkomała and Belomorkanalskaya did "*Sto lat*" in Polish—I noticed that Zekovich joined them in wishing a hundred years of life to himself—and then Wirrwarr launched into an off-tone version of "*Hoch soll er leben*!" Mercifully, the mellifluous Heldenplatz joined in and by, outdoing her in volume, transformed it into a tolerable melody. When the singing was over, it was Zekovich's turn to say something. He rose slowly to his feet, tottered a bit, and said, "Senk you, senk you, dir friends." Then he gave Dickey and Joe bear hugs and turned back to the crowd and flashed a V-sign. It occurred to me that "Senk you, senk you, dir friends" was probably all the English he knew.

"And now," Dickey beamed, "a spot of bubbly, what?" The waiters had wheeled in tray carts with champagne flutes filled to the brim. "Much to celebrate. Much to toast. A job bloody well done!" The glasses were distributed and Dickey continued. "A bloody toast to bloody us!" A series of hear-hears and hurrahs ensued and the manic clinking that followed resembled the clicking of the cicadas. "To us! To us!" individual voices cried. "To us!" I downed my champagne and quickly grabbed another flute from the cart. The hubbub was decreasing in proportion to the amount of bubbly being consumed; the meeting was breaking up. I was about to go outside for some fresh air, when I caught sight of Dickey hailing me.

"I say, ole boy! I say, Chester! A word with the president, what?"

Zekovich had an unusually strong grip, like that of a boxer or wrestler. He pumped my hand several times and wouldn't let go, looking me straight in the eyes and saying "Senk you, senk you, dir friend." At least his knowledge of English involved recognition of the difference between the singular and plural form of nouns—or, more correctly, of one noun. I almost said "Senk you" as well, but changed course just as he released his hold and simply thanked him. He mumbled something in the direction of his gray-suited translator, who smiled obsequiously and said: "Prezeedent Zekoveech veeshes to thank you perso-NAH-lly for parteeceepating in EEM-potent meeting. Prezeedent Zekoveech is believing demo-CRA-cy and market E-conomy is needing poyetry for pipple." Zekovich resumed his mumbling. "And Prezeedent Zekoveech is extending een-vee-tay-shoon to esteemed Nobel Prize lau-re-AHT to veezeet his beauteefool cown-tree on prezeedenshool jet."

"The presidential jet?" Well, well, well! I was, frankly, taken aback. Friday-afternoon lunches at the president's digs were one thing. This was something altogether different. I had, in the bat of an eyelash, been catapulted from the minors to the majors.

"Good show, ole boy!" Dickey chimed in like a canary. "Made quite an impression on the president, what? Could be quite a junket. Interesting, lucrative, and all that. Might want to give it a thought, eh?"

"When?" I blurted. (Sadly, that is exactly what I did: blurt.) Why did I say yes so quickly? In order to assert my contrarianism by confounding Dickey and his implication that I wouldn't go? Or was it because I had never been to Zekovich's part of the world and a jaunt in a jet might prove to be a kick?

"Tomorrow," the interpreter said. "Ahf-ter conference ends."

"Sure." What else could I say?

"Vee take khelicopter to Milano, then prezeedenshool jet. One, two, tree: vee are khome! Een prezeedenshool pa-LAHTS. Very beauteefool."

"Been there once, ole boy. High class, top of the line, top of the shelf. A chateau, actually. Once occupied by a bloody king. Or was it a czar? Bloody high class either way. Won't find a nigger in his woodpile, ole boy."

"Sure," I repeated. "I'll be packed and ready to go in the afternoon." With hindsight, I can only plead a temporary suspension of my moral faculties. Why, I don't know, but it hadn't yet dawned on me that I might be selling my gentle soul to a Eurasian Beelzebub. Perhaps the terseness of my usually more expansive speech was a subliminal sign that, subconsciously, I was fully aware that something was off kilter. Or is this just an ex post facto rationalization? Who knows?

Zekovich seized my limp hand and began pumping it like the rusty handle of an ancient artesian well. I smiled and, not unexpectedly, he cried, "Senk you, senk you, dir friend!" This time, I kept pumping even when I felt he was ready to stop. He looked momentarily confused. Then, clarity illuminated his face and he pulled me to himself and wrapped his huge arms around me. "Senk you, senk you, *tovarishch!*" With my face pressed against Zekovich's pounding breast, I could hardly breathe; my glasses rested crookedly on my nose, but I could see Dickey and he was winking in evident approval. "Quite a coup, ole boy, quite a bloody coup," he whispered. "Played bloody well—bloody damned well! Thought you were just a bloody good poet! Still waters run bloody deep, eh?"

***

Dickey's reference to still waters stayed with me even after I escaped Zekovich's embrace and fled to the least populated part of the boat, the front. (Is that the bow or the stern?) The sun was setting behind the mountains, their edges blurred by an orange glow. A strong headwind blew and, like a thirsty traveler at an oasis, I gulped down the cool air. The boat was moving several miles per hour—does anyone know what a nautical knot is and why sailors use knots instead of miles?—and was slicing through the inky water, leaving two trails of sparkling jewels and cream. On shore, some street lamps had already been illuminated and the light they cast seemed to radiate inward. We were on the dark side of the promontory; Caravaggio, its white and ochre buildings shimmering in the dying sunlight, lay to the right. After a few minutes my head felt clear again—or clear enough to embark on a bit of cogitation.

It was time to take stock. (Again! How times had I taken stock already? And to what avail?) I had just accepted an invitation from a corrupt dictator and would be traveling with him in the lap of luxury (the term was quite appropriate) to his lair (another quite appropriate term with, *nota bene*, obvious implications of bestiality). Once there, he would presumably parade me, like a peacock, before his colleagues, crooks, and cronies and show me off to the pipple as proof of the benevolent nature of his rule. I'd be wined and dined. They'd shower me with gifts. (Once again, I felt the hackneyed phrases best captured my hackneyed situation.) They'd probably shower me with girls. (See how the unexpected juxtaposition of a cliché with a simple observation statement can produce an interesting effect?) By the time it was all over, I might be compromised—ethically, morally, professionally. I could visualize the slippery slope ending abruptly in a quick leap off a short pier.

Or, then again, I might not. If I let them compromise me, I would be compromised. But if I didn't let them compromise me, I would not be compromised. My logic was impeccable and unassailable. It all depended on me, did it not? If I remained strong—and why shouldn't I? I was a poet, after all—all would be well. If I became weak—and there was nothing in my past or present behavior to suggest that I would abandon all my principles at the drop of a hat, a pin, or a shoe—then all would be lost. In a word, I would remain strong and not become weak. It was as simple as that. And, in the process, I would have a remarkable adventure. What could possibly be wrong with that?

Now, granted, rubbing elbows (Lord! Another cliché!) with dictators might rub off on me, even if I remained on guard all the time. As someone who had slid across a buffet table, I could speak with experience about slippery slopes. But didn't that analogy just demonstrate that all would be well? After all, just what happened to me after my encounter with the canapés? I had a few mayonnaise smudges on my shirt and shorts, but they were nothing to write home about and nothing that couldn't be easily removed with a spot of salt and cold water. And yes, I had some mustard in my nostrils and right ear. A few deft wipes of my wet handkerchief and that problem was settled as well. Didn't I just need to have the ethical equivalent of cold water, salt, and a wet handkerchief on hand during my trip to Zekovich's den? That seemed easy enough, even to a poet. I took a deep breath of the intoxicating air. I had made up my mind and had no qualms. I would be a guest of President Viktor Illich Zekovich. Damn the torpedoes! Full steam ahead! But wait! Wasn't his country land-locked?

***

The footsteps on the deck behind me belonged to Louise, Thor, and Serge—all splendidly drunk and quite visibly amused by something. And—O frabjous day! Callooh! Callay!—they were all clothed. Babylon was wearing a tight (frankly, too tight, given her proportions) knee-length black skirt and red silk blouse with, naturally, her usual torpedo bra (that, however mismatched, did have the distinct advantage of containing her oversized mammary glands); her lips glowed, her hair was collected in a donut, and her earlobes sported two-inch wide bangles. Kriegman had donned a beige Seersucker suit, white cotton shirt, and (unnecessarily, I thought) an ascot (polyester or silk?). Joupanencoff had opted for torn jeans, a linen jacket, a black shirt (I couldn't tell whether it was linen or cotton, but knew instinctively it couldn't be polyester), and, for the *coup de grâce*, a silk scarf, which he had wound several times around his neck, loosely, almost carelessly, so as to create the effect of bored indifference, of course. With the sun behind my back, they were unlikely to see the mayonnaise stains on my shirt.

"The poet stands above the mighty roar of the ocean and contemplates infinity!" It was Kriegman. Who else would try to imitate Pericles?

"Well, not exactly."

"Out, out, brief candle! Life is but a—what? Louise, how does the rest go, Louise?"

"A poor player, I think."

"No, there's something before that. A shadow?"

"A walking shadow," I said.

"Exactly!" Thor cried. "Life is but a walking shadow and a poor player who—"

"That," I corrected him.

"That? But that's wrong! A player *who*: shouldn't it be a player *who*?"

"Maybe," I said. "But it's *that* in the text."

"Very well, we'll go with your version: a poor player who, I mean, that struts and frets his hour upon the stage—"

"End zen eez 'eard no more," Joupanencoff finished the line and sniffed.

"Bravo, *monsieur le acteur*! Bravo Sir Poet! And," he made a deep bow, "bravo to me too. I may be a mere journalist, a mere best-selling author, but—"

"Stop, *idiot: arrête!*" Louise snapped. "You can be so infuriating." This time, the image of a mousetrap came to mind. She turned to me. "Where have you been all day? Taking a nap, I heard. You missed all the fun. By the way, we have something fabulous"—she extended the first syllable for about two beats—"to tell you, something that'll make you drool with envy."

"Should we tell?" Kriegman giggled like a schoolgirl. "Should we really?"

"Eh, *bien sûr*!" Joupanencoff said. "*Pourqois pas*? We ahr all franz, no? *Monsieur le poète* must know everyseeng!"

"Know what?" I said.

"Tomorrow," Louise announced, "the three of us will be boarding the presidential helicopter and flying to Malpensa airport. Now get this. There we'll board the presidential jet and fly to—"

"Me too."

"What do you mean me too?"

"I'll be on the same helicopter and the same jet."

"Zekovich invited you as well?" Louise seemed shocked and not a bit disappointed by the news.

"I guess so," I replied with all the silken insouciance I could spin. "How could he pass up the opportunity to host a Nobel Prize winner at his palace?"

"Why that's wonderful!" Thor appeared genuinely enthused. "The more, the merrier. I hear they've got excellent vodkas—world class stuff. And they'll probably feed us well too."

"Oh, shut up," she snapped (the verb, however tired from overuse, really did fit: in any case, I couldn't think of anything else at that particular moment). "You're just an idiot, full of sound and fury—"

"*Je sais, je sais!*" Joupanencoff cried. "SeegneefyEENG nah-SEENG!"

"*Idiot*!"

"And what will you be doing there?" I resolved to defuse the tension and calm La Babylon's nerves. "Did they tell you?"

Thor: "Not a word."

Louise: "Who cares?"

Serge: "*Exactement!* 'oo cares?"

"Aren't you disturbed by his dictatorial proclivities?" I have no idea why I said that.

Louise: "Are you?"

Thor: "No."

Serge: "*Qu'est-ce que c'est*—pro-clee-vee-TEEZ?"

"Or that he'll probably use us?" I continued with my role of devil's advocate.

Thor (firmly): "Let him. I intend to use him."

Serge (hotly): "I am *un acteur*, not *un politicien*."

Louise (coolly): "*Idiot!* You can be so infuriating!"

I realized, just as she finished saying ee-dee-O, that I had purposely, if unconsciously, provoked her so as to elicit that lovely vowel-and-consonant combination. How remarkable, how stupendous, how positively splendid that the sound of a word should contradict its meaning! Was there a word for anti-onomatopoeia? Was there even a philosophical discussion of this fascinating linguistic phenomenon? Had I, perhaps, inadvertently stumbled upon one of those rare insights that lead to breakthroughs in knowledge? Had I discovered a Big Idea that could revolutionize the world (as well as reduce Thor's obsession with flatness to epistemological dust)? Were my somnolent Muses trying to tell me something? Was this their coy way of expressing approval of my decision to embark on my zekovichian adventure? *Si, si*, and once again *si*!

It dawned on me that the confusion over my identity had not been accidental. To be sure, Joe Zsasz and Dickey Lemon truly believed they had invited Czesław Milosz. They had obviously not *really* intended for me to come. But, whatever their intent, the fact of the matter was that I had been the one to receive the invitation and that I had come—both as Chess-wow and as Czesław. I hadn't changed a whit, but I had in fact become two people—myself and the other Milosz. And that couldn't be an accident. That couldn't be a random occurrence or the product of some serendipitous confluence of contingent events. After all, why did they want to invite Czesław? His presence at Ardor Haus made no more sense than mine. Somehow, somewhy, someone had made that decision. And then somehow, somewhy, someone made the decision to invite me. And here I was—Chess-wow/Czesław, the only man in the world who had simultaneously won, not won, and would win the Nobel Prize! There was obviously some larger purpose at work here. The hand of God? Maybe. The hand of Art? Why not? The hand of History? Could be. Or had God, Art, and History conspired to bring me to the shores of Lago Caravaggio in the hope that I would carry out some special mission? The evidence was all circumstantial and speculative, but I was, to quote the venerable Dickey Lemon, bloody damned sure that something bloody damned big was bloody damned afoot.

"Very well," I responded to the threesome, "we will all leave tomorrow together. Did they tell you what time?"

Louise (remotely): "No."

Serge (also remotely): "*Mais non.*"

Thor (authoritatively): "After lunch, I assume. Those boys are big eaters and I can't imagine their leaving before the big spread."

"I suggest," I continued, "that we put our heads together and develop a plan of action—so that we spend our time there as productively as possible."

Serge (distractedly): "I need a dreenk."

Louise (lividly): "You can be such a bore."

Thor (constructively): "Let's do that on the plane from Milano. Meanwhile, how about some champagne, Louise?"

With that, the three flew away and I remained standing at the railing again, alone. Which was just as well, actually, as they had been distracting me from my ruminations. Very well, then, I thought: let's assume I was here with a purpose, and a big purpose at that. Just what could that purpose be? To save the world? Not my line of work. To make money? I wasn't interested. To network? What a bore. There was only one thing left: to write poetry! That had to be it. I was here because the Muses had willed it. I was here to find creative fulfillment. I was here to produce earthshattering poetry. I was here to break conceptual barriers and create verbal tsunamis. I was here to win the Prize. It was—it had to be—as simple as that. Chester Milosz had been confused with Czesław Milosz for a reason. And that reason was this: Chester Milosz was to follow in Czesław Milosz's footsteps to Oslo!

***

As I was returning to the buffet, Dickey grabbed my elbow and pulled me to the side. He handed me a large cognac, wished me good health, and quickly downed his. His face was flushed, his hair was disheveled, and his eyes had the glassy glow that usually lit up faculty Christmas parties. He was breathing heavily and he slurred his words, though just barely.

"Big man likes you, ole boy. Made quite an impression on him. Not easy, you know. Not bloody easy at all. Has shtandards. Knows the ways of the world. Recognizes a nigger in the woodpile when he shees one. Can't fool him, ole boy. Can't fool him at all. Shmart, you know? Bloody damned shmart. Not as shmart as Joe, of course: no one is. But bloody damned shmart. Cheers, ole boy! Top it off, eh? Never had much of an education, the president. Not like you and me. Shtreet urchin, teenage tough, and all that. Arrested once or twice. Shurprised? Don't be, ole boy. Happens to the best of them. Joe did the arresting. The president was arrested. Ironic, what? Bloody damned ironic I'd say. Theft, minor shtuff. Shome say rape or attempted rape. Blood big difference, what? Shat a few years. Learned the ropes. Learned to be a big man. Feels angry? Feels resentful? Not a bit, not a bloody bit. Put it all behind him. Picked himshelf up. Moved on. Top of the world now, eh? Top of the bloody world. And, ole boy, likes you, likes you bloody damned a lot. The poetry, what? The poet, eh? The poet and his poetry! I say, ole boy, no shtopping you now. It's up, up, and away. Shky's the limit and all that. Have another drink? Word of warning, ole chap. Big man's a shtraight shooter. Doesn't like guff. Punch in the nose, eh? Not a good thing, ole boy, not a bloody good thing."

"Thanks for the advice, Dickey."

"Not to worry, ole boy, ole Dickey'll be there. Hold your hand, offer a shoulder, and all that. Joe too. Bloody genius that Joe, what? Bloody, bloody genius. Wouldn't be here without him. No one would. You too, ole boy. Well, cheers, ole boy! To your health, to my health, to our health, and all that. A few shkeletons in his closet, a corpse or two in the backyard, but who doesn't, eh? No shaints here, what? All shinners. Never could understand the difference between venial shins and mortal shins. You? Shin is a shin, what? Joe's a shinner. Big man's a shinner. You, me, the whole lot, eh? The whole world. Nigger in the woodpile, I say. Doesn't pay the rent, eh? Doesn't leave a tip or cook dinner, right? No use for shin, ole boy. Let the priests keep it. Gives them shomething to live for. Fix the world, I say, make it shafe for democrashy, and all that. Our job, eh? Our mission, right, ole boy?"

"Right."

"Leave tomorrow after lunch. Bit tight in the copter. Lap of luxury in the plane. Big, shpacious, shtretch out your legs, take a walk. Fabulous food, shplendid wines. Big man knows how to live. Sho does Joe. Bloody genius that Joe, bloody, bloody genius. Have another drink? No? Don't mind me if I do. Good night, ole boy. Careful with La Babylon. Lady's a viper. Shlept with the whole boat, I dare shay. Has a poishonous bite, if you know what I mean."

Before I could respond, Dickey did a pirouette and shtumbled away.

***

We disembarked in town at around nine o'clock. The promenade was packed, as were the restaurants and cafés. The lanterns glowed like diamonds against the dark blue sky and the clashing smells of perfume, sweat, fish, alcohol, and coffee commingled to produce the intoxicating effect of a slightly rancid spice bazaar. Some of our group decided to have another drink; I joined those who headed for the villa. The hike through the underbrush, the heat, the crash, the water, the buffet table—and then, to top it all off, the tête-à-tête with Zekovich—were too much for my frazzled nerves. I was, in a word, ready to collapse: in the gutter, if necessary, into bed, if possible. As we turned into a pitch-black alley, a hand took mine and wet lips brushed against my ear. "My room, tonight," I heard Louise whisper. And then, just as suddenly, the hands and lips were gone. When we emerged into a brightly lit street, she was nowhere to be seen. Instead, Orestes Heldenplatz, the Argentinian weapons specialist, was walking alongside me and whistling a vaguely familiar tune.

"I know that melody," I said hazily, "but can't quite pin it down."

"*Lili Marleen,*" he answered. "My father, bless his soul, used to sing it all the time."

"From the war?"

"*Sonderkommando.*" He sighed. "It scarred him for life. After the capitulation, he came to Argentina to seek a new life, to be reborn."

"Did he find it? A new life, I mean."

"*Si.* He even changed his name to mark the new beginning. Have jou been to my country, señor? It is the true new world. Jou should come someday. I would be honored and delighted to host jou. My wife Brunnhilde is one of jour greatest admirers. She knows many of jour poems by heart."

"I'll be sure to take you up on that."

"Do you dance, señor?"

"A bit."

"My Brunnhilde is a magnificent tango dancer. She does an incredible Milonga, one that will literally leave jou breathless, señor." Heldenplatz's use of my own overworked adverb was a nice touch. Was there more to him than met the eye?

"I'm afraid I only know some very elementary tango steps."

"Then my Brunnhilde will teach jou the Argentine tango! It is a very special dance, señor."

"The vertical expression of a horizontal longing, I believe."

"How is that? The vertical expression—oh, I see! Very clever,

Señor Miloss, very, very clever. I shall have to tell Brunnhilde. The vertical—how did you put it? Ah, yes! The vertical expression of horizontal longings! Very, very clever, Señor Miloss! A true poet! A true master of language! Bravo! Bravissimo! Brunnhilde will find jou most amusing! How was it again? The horizontal expression of—? Oh, *meine* Brunnhilde will find jou most amusing!"

FIVE

C. Milosz almost gets to travel in a presidential jet and reside in a palace, survives a major earthquake, and finally finds inspiration on the rooftop of the Duomo

I confess to having toyed very, very briefly with the idea of visiting Louise's room, but my overripe sense of self-preservation easily prevailed and I headed straight for my room. I kept the light turned off and retreated into the spacious bathroom and shut the door. I even placed a wet towel along the crack on the floor. Then I filled the bathtub with lukewarm water and climbed in. If she knocked, I wouldn't hear and she wouldn't know I was inside. With a little luck, she might decide I had stayed behind in town. And if she kept on knocking, I would in all likelihood remain blissfully unaware. My only regret was not hearing the inevitable string of ee-dee-Os.

Besides, I desperately needed a good bath. My plunges into Lago Caravaggio and the opulent buffet table had left me bruised and dirty, while my repeated elbow-rubbing with the rich and mighty required a ritual purification. Alcohol helped, but it hadn't quite dulled my feeling of moral decay. I held my breath and submerged my head. How long could I stay underwater? A minute? Two at the most? What if I just swam away? I exhaled and emerged, the water running down my face like torrents of tears. A distant banging on the door interrupted my reverie. It was a red-faced Louise, I hoped. Perhaps if I submerged my head again, it—she—would go away. A minute or two later, I surfaced, only to hear the banging again. She wouldn't be this persistent. La Babylon would rap on the door a few times, make her point, and then storm away. Should I escape underwater or go on land and answer the door? The question answered itself. I donned the bathrobe Ardor Haus had so kindly provided and tapped my way along the marble floor. I resisted the urge to yank open the door and, instead, placed my eye to the peephole. To my surprise it was Zekovich.

"Senk you," he blubbered, obviously quite drunk, when I opened the door. "Senk you, dir friend." He was standing in a sleeveless undershirt and large, as well as noticeably soiled, underpants. I smiled.

"You my friend?" he asked timidly.

"Yes, I your friend." Was this a homosexual come-on? I had heard of repressed authoritarians who denied their sexuality with exaggerated displays of machismo—like the diminutive president of Russia.

"Senk you, senk you." He appeared to want to hug me, but I drew back instinctively.

"You're welcome."

"Vodka?"

"No, thank you," I said, "no more for me today." He appeared puzzled at first. Then, for the second time in a few hours, a look of clarity enveloped his massive face. I was, evidently, the bearer of epiphanies for him.

"No, no, no! No VEES-per een khowl of HE-sto-ree?" he giggled like a schoolgirl. "Vodka for Viktor Zekovich!" Had he been knocking on all the doors or had he specifically come to me? I suddenly had an inspired idea.

"There." I pointed to Louise's door across the hall. "There. There is vodka. There you will find a whisper in the howl of history." More like a bloody howl in the bloody whisper of history, I thought.

"MEH-nee?"

"Oh, yes, very many vodka," I assured him with a slap on his back. As he stumbled forward, I noticed that the seat of his undershorts was also soiled. I couldn't resist a malevolent smile: Louise would be delighted by his appearance.

***

I wasn't disappointed. Next day at breakfast the first thing Louise said to me as she threw her plate on the table was, of course, "ee-dee-O!" I feigned both ignorance and innocence. She went on to berate me for having foisted the insufferable Ze-KO-vich on her. Had I no decency? Had I purposely slighted her? Did I want to add insult to the injury of rejecting her proposition? Why was I as insufferable as the insufferable Ze-KO-vich? Why was I an ee-dee-O as much as he was? Didn't I have any decency? Did I purposely slight her? It was at this point, when she began to repeat herself, that I stopped listening, assumed a look of blissful unawareness, and nodded—whether wisely or in assent was for her to decide: I had no idea. As I expected, every time she said ee-dee-O, I shivered (literally) with delight. Maintaining that blissfully unaware pose while shivering (literally) was not, I can assure you, a piece of cake.

"Finished?" I smiled. "You know, I have absolutely no idea what you're talking about. Really."

"Ee-dee-O! You can be so insufferable." Ah, I thought: The *terremoto* has abated. Conversation might be possible again.

"Have you packed? All ready for the big trip?" I couldn't resist. "Packed your clean undies?"

"Ee-dee-O," she snickered. "Were they yours?"

"What were mine?"

"The dirty shorts—when we arrived. They were yours, weren't they?"

"You noticed!"

"Of course I noticed. Everybody did."

"But no one said anything."

"Of course they didn't. This is Europe, ee-dee-O."

"I wear cheap jockey shorts," I said. "Those were Dickey's. His exact brand. His exact size."

"How would you know? Have you two been…?"

"He gave me a clean pair on the boat, after I fell in the water." Again, I couldn't resist. "Shouldn't *you* know? Weren't the two of you an item once upon a time?"

"You can be so insufferable," she sighed. "Is that how you get your inspiration? From underwear?"

"We Nobel Prize-winning poets see and hear everything, my dear." I decided to adopt a paternalistic tone. "Everything, no matter how small, no matter how dirty, can provide the inspiration for a work of genius." This was too much, I knew, but what had I to lose? To my astonishment, Louise took the bait.

"Why yes, my thoughts exactly!" she gushed (literally). "I've always considered that the ontological sources of both science and art can be found in the quotidian reality of phenomenological existence." And on she went in that vein. Once again, with reality repeating itself before my very eyes, I decided to repeat my earlier response and my description of that response—thereby adding two layers of déjà vu to the actual sensation of déjà vu. Once again, I stopped listening, assumed a look of blissful unawareness, and nodded—whether wisely or in assent was for her to decide: I had no idea.

I still recall exactly that it happened at the precise moment Louise said the word "epistemology." Indeed, it happened just as the last syllable escaped her lips. The floor and walls and ceiling shook, the china rattled, and a deep rumble emerged from within the bowels of the earth. This was no tremor, I immediately realized. This was a full-blown *terremoto*. I seized her hand and, despite her protestations that she hadn't finished her thought, led her, while she exclaimed ee-dee-O with every reluctant step, outside. Structures were unsafe. So were, I supposed, trees. I dragged her to the middle of the parking area, where a crowd of panic-stricken people were already milling about. The late risers were still in their pajamas, bathrobes, or underclothes. Some were lying face down on the gravel, their hands over their heads. A huge crack had appeared in the side of the villa. Another rumble followed and the earth swayed. The crack grew larger and, suddenly, as we watched, part of the tile roof caved in above the reception area. One of the personnel emerged, covered in white dust, coughing. I heard Louise say, "This can be so infuriating," and then dive to the ground where the other bodies lay.

I decided to withdraw up the road leading from the gate to the villa, where the vantage point was better. I was terrified, but I was also exhilarated and I didn't want to miss anything. In town, several of the buildings nearest the gate had collapsed and clouds of gray dust swirled above them. Large waves jostled one another on the crazily rippled lake. And then, from behind the villa there rose, its propellers chopping the turbulent air, Zekovich's helicopter. I could see him through the glass. He appeared to be wearing the same undershirt he had on last night. The helicopter hovered above the cypress trees momentarily—and as it did I thought I glimpsed Joe, Dickey, and Stefan von Troubadour as well—and then shot in the direction of the lake. There went my trip to the president's miserable cown-tree.

***

Half an hour later, the earthquake was over. The villa still stood, although several new cracks had appeared, crisscrossing the walls like spider webs, and more of the front roof had fallen in. The stillness was nothing less than—pardon the cliché—eerie. We stood, hands and knees trembling, eyes squinting, nostrils flared, waiting, for five minutes, for ten, for fifteen, but nothing more happened. The cicadas resumed their buzzing. A strong wind blew, bending the cypresses and sending white-capped wavelets across the lake. As we became accustomed to the quiet, we also became aware, quite unexpectedly, of the wailing and crying wafting toward us from Caravaggio and from within Ardor Haus. I shocked myself by taking the initiative and heading for the villa. Bravery was not exactly one of my strong points and, although I liked to think I had as much compassion as the other guy, it rarely reared its head at times of danger.

"We have to look for survivors—inside. Who'll come with me? Thor, you. Roach? Heldenplatz? And you, Palermo."

Kriegman, Heldenplatz, and Palermo joined me, while Roach begged off. "A knock on the head—can't." He spoke breathlessly, as if he had just been running and not lying in the ground. "Wish I could—honest."

"Sexist swine," Louise said and poked her forefinger in my chest. "Count me in."

We entered the vestibule, carefully stepping over the rubble and holding our handkerchiefs to our noses and mouths. The air was dense with a white powder—plaster, concrete, or asbestos perhaps? One of the maids, her face an alabaster white, was sitting on the red-carpeted staircase, crying, but otherwise unharmed. The Otto Room and the Nikolai Room were untouched. The breakfast buffet was a mess: rolls, croissants, pastries, bread loaves, meats, cereals, jams, fish, and condiments lay in a jumble on the tables and the floor, along with the coffee pots and jugs of juice. The Argentinian grabbed a croissant and stuffed it into his mouth. "Excuse me," he mumbled in between chews, "but I had no breakfast." The tables in the seminar room had shifted, from the square in which they had been arranged to something resembling a rhombus. Pellegrino, Fanta, and Coca-Cola bottles were scattered among the papers, pencils, and microphones on the marble floor. When we stepped through the glass doors onto the lawn, we found the staff and three members of our group—Balletmeister, de Pouff, and La Baguette.

"Are all your people safe?" I asked the headwaiter.

"One girl is missing. A maid."

"She's inside. She's safe." It was then that I noticed three of Zekovich's gray suits milling about. One of them was the translator. "Why didn't you leave with your president?" I asked. "I saw the helicopter departing just after the first shock."

"Prezeedent and com-RAYDS must be lea-veenk very queeckly." I noticed a trace of bitterness in his voice. "Very EEM-potent pipple."

"But you are his translator!"

"Very EEM-potent pipple," he repeated. "We"—and he pointed

to himself and his two colleagues—"not very EEM-potent pipple." His voice assumed a tone of resignation. "And dat eez dat."

"In the helicopter, with him, I mean, those were Joe Zsasz, Dickey—"

"—Lay-mon and Meester von Troubadour. Yes. Very EEM-potent pipple. We go have breakfast now, OK?"

I shrugged. So I was right: Zekovich, Joe, Dickey, and their lawyer had hightailed it out of here. The meeting of great minds was definitely over. I decided to follow the translator to the Otto Room. A croissant, even a stale one shaken and stirred by an earthquake, looked good.

"Wait!" It was Palermo. "My Mercedes is parked outside. I suggest the five of us leave as quickly as possible. We can be in Milano by nightfall at the latest."

"I'm packed," I announced.

"So am I," said Thor and Louise.

"I too am ready to depart," Heldenplatz added.

"Then we meet at my car in exactly fifteen minutes. No fanfare, *please,* no extended good-byes, no hearty handshakes, no tearful farewells. We want to make a quick exit and not cause a commotion or attract attention. Are we in agreement, my friends? In exactly fifteen minutes I turn the key and start the ignition and we leave. If you are not there, you will not come with us. Understood?"

Impressed by the little man's authoritative tone, we nodded and rushed off. On the way, I wrapped several croissants in a large white linen napkin, popped a roll of extra-spicy Matjes herring into my mouth, and took a quick swig from the open champagne bottle. It would be a long day and who knew whether there'd be any functioning restaurants on the way to the big city.

***

We made our way through the debris-strewn streets of Caravaggio; I sat in the front with Palermo, the others were in the back. Many buildings had been reduced to rubble. Wooden beams, red bricks, cinderblocks, cement, and plaster lay in jagged heaps to our left and right. The wailing of police and ambulance sirens mixed with shouts and cries and crying. Knots of desperate-looking men and women scurried along the streets. The town looked like it had just undergone a sustained bombardment. His eyes bulging, Palermo drove in fits and starts, honking incessantly and cursing both the debris and whoever crossed our path.

"Shouldn't we stop and help?" Thor suggested. "I've been to war zones, but this—"

"No," Palermo replied flatly and accelerated before pressing on the brakes. "I must get back to the ministry."

"Not for long," Kriegman persisted. "Just a half hour."

"That will make no difference. If you want to get out, please do so. Otherwise, we continue." Thor said nothing in response.

A lantern had fallen across the street and we had to turn into an alley on the left. Remarkably, the houses on both sides were intact for about one hundred yards and we zoomed along until we reached an intersection where an ambulance, its red lights flashing, stood amid the rising dust of collapsed houses. Orderlies with stretchers and medical kits were climbing the rubble and a policeman produced a piercing whistle and ordered us to stop. We jerked to a halt and Palermo, cursing, jumped out of the Mercedes and approached the officer, waving a document and passport at him. His golf-ball eyes looked exceptionally large and threatening. A brief conversation followed, Palermo placed something into the man's vest pocket, and he smiled sheepishly. As Palermo returned to the car, the policeman spoke to the ambulance driver and the vehicle advanced a yard or two, opening up just enough space for us to squeeze through at a snail's pace.

"Very impressive," I said. "What did you show him?"

"Nothing," Palermo grunted, his mood quite evidently still foul. "He understood the gravity of our situation and proved quite amenable to compromise."

"You bribed him," Louise said.

"Naturally. That is the only language these people understand."

The promenade and its establishments appeared to have survived intact. The cafés were full of gesticulating men sipping espressos, while the women and children, some fully dressed, some in their night clothes, stood along the railing near the lake. The traffic was heavy and the pedestrians crowded the streets; we had to get in line behind scores of other slow-moving vehicles escaping the *terremoto*. The sky, absurdly, was a cloudlessly gorgeous azure blue, as if it were declaring its indifference to what had just transpired or its confidence that all would be well. Not a single boat could be seen on the lake. Many of the buildings dotting the shore, however, had been damaged. How severe had the destruction been in the towns between here and Milano?

"This country needs a Peron," Heldenplatz said, his forefinger raised.

"If you mean Evita," Louise countered, "you're right."

"I meant Juan, of course." He paused for a second. His sense of irony, like La Babylon's, was minimal. "A great man. He made my country great. He could make this country great."

"I suppose next you'll be defending Mussolini." Louise spoke angrily this time and I knew that, unless I intervened, the conversation would spiral out of control. I recalled my raid of the buffet that morning.

"Croissants, anyone? I took a few before we left. Señor? Louise?" They grabbed the flattened pieces of moist dough greedily. The conversation ended. My peacemaking expedition had been successful and, as we crawled along the promenade, I returned to observing life outside the Mercedes. I should have known better. Louise had different plans in mind.

"So," she said while chewing on her croissant, "so, Thor, tell me something. Does the earthquake vindicate your ideas about flatness? I mean, look around you. It's all flat, leveled—a moonscape. Just as you predicted, *n'est çe pas*?" I resisted the urge to turn around and glare at her; Thor said nothing. "I mean, seriously, Thor," she continued, undeterred by our silence, "it doesn't get any flatter than this, does it?" This time Heldenplatz, who clearly managed to understand Louise far more quickly than I had, intervened.

"All in all, the conference was, I think, a big success. Don't jou agree? Our minds were enriched, our pockets were enriched, and our bellies were enriched. Very well: the earthquake intervened, but I think we all accomplished what we set out to accomplish. Am I not right, Señor Miloss?"

"Oh, absolutely," I said quietly.

"Have jou been inspired to write more magnificent poetry? Have I told jou that I am a great admirer—perhaps Argentina's greatest—of jour poetry? I have been reading jou faithfully since my university days in Buenos Aires. Argentina is a country of lovers—and of lovers of poetry, señor. Your collections adorn every educated person's book shelves."

"You flatter me, señor. As to inspiration"—I decided to be Delphic in my pronouncements—"everything inspires me and nothing inspires me. Inspiration comes from—"

"—God, señor?"

"From the devil," Louise muttered, "is more likely."

"Exactly, señor," I declared with all the authority I could summon. "Inspiration is divine."

The others fell silent. After all, what could they say to so crushing a banality? I had learned that technique in classrooms and at conferences. Naturally, it mattered what you said. But far more important was how you said it. Say something silly with self-confidence and force, as if you were revealing a profound truth, and most people will believe you and those that do not will be too cowed by the universally nodding heads to protest. I had always thought that this sheep-like behavior was unique to my world. As Ardor Haus taught me, it could be found everywhere. Indeed, the so-called real world's willingness to kowtow to stupidity was significantly greater than ours. We academics occasionally had bad consciences; the denizens of the real world just happily, willfully, and obliviously followed the money—*any* money—anywhere (and I mean anywhere) at all.

"*Si*, señor," Heldenplatz finally broke the silence, "verily it is."

"Verily!" Louise exploded like a firecracker. "He actually said verily! Do you think this is Elizabethan England? Ee-dee-O!"

I expected Heldenplatz to respond in kind, but, instead, he smiled obsequiously and said, "Please forgive my infelicities, Professor Babylon, but English is, alas, my eighth language and I fully admit to speaking it most imperfectly." Bravo, Orestes! I thought. A perfect rejoinder. What would she say?

"Do we have any more croissants?" Louise barked (the word is exactly appropriate; in any case, I can assure you she did not purr, as might have been more appropriate for an apologetic tone). "I'm starved. How about stopping for lunch?"

"As soon as we leave this miserable town, Madame," Palermo said as we approached the road that would take us out of Caravaggio and into the mountains, "that is the first thing we shall do." He made a left and, although the traffic was still heavy, we were able to climb the hill at about twenty miles per hour. The earthquake had struck hard the buildings on both sides of the road. What remained of them, mostly crumbling walls, resembled bombed-out ruins. The ambulances had not yet reached this part of town and scores of dazed and wounded people lined the road, some standing aimlessly, most sitting on the grass or rubble. A man stood, crying, with the broken body of a child in his arms. A woman, indifferent to the oncoming cars, stumbled onto the road, paused briefly, and shuffled to the other side where she collapsed under a tree. Palermo accelerated and we spurted forward until, once again, he braked suddenly and we all jerked forward.

"Whoa, cowboy!" Kriegman cried. "Why don't you hold your horses, podner?" Palermo ignored him and gave the car more gas.

"Hey, slow down: we're liable to hit someone."

"In my car," Palermo replied testily, "I drive. If you like, I can stop and you may walk. That is your choice." Did little Svven have a Napoleon complex?

"No need to lose your temper, podner," Kriegman said. "Your car, your show." Once again, Heldenplatz deftly intervened.

"As I was saying, my friends, the conference was a huge success."

"That Zekovich," Palermo murmured in approval, "is a brilliant man. My only regret is that we couldn't continue our conversation today."

"What will jou tell jour ministry?" Heldenplatz asked.

"The same as you will tell yours." He pressed the horn and honked at a car that was backing out of a driveway. "These Italians can be idiots."

"I will recommend signing the contracts immediately—of course."

"Ditto for me," Palermo said. "This is a once-in-a-lifetime opportunity: no responsible government can forego it."

"What *are* you boys talking about?" Louise said with the sweetness of a vanilla sundae. "Deals, opportunities! My, my, one would think we've just been at a business meeting."

"You know quite well," Palermo turned his head briefly and reproached her. "I dare say you know better than any of us." Now *I* was completely puzzled. (Again, you will say.) What possible relationship could La Babylon have to the multimillion-dollar deals the two had been talking about? True, she and Thor had been on the boat when I had had my unfortunate mishap. They had been there for a purpose. They had been invited. Were they in the inner circle? Of course they were. I had concluded that then, when I was on board. Why should I be surprised to see the obvious now? I decided to take the bull by the horns (a silly expression that, in this case, was quite apposite considering the trepidation I felt in approaching a livid Louise).

"Both of you may know, but we don't. In any case, I don't and I'm a Nobel Prize winner. What's the big secret, Louise? Come, tell all—perhaps it'll inspire a new poem."

"There's nothing to tell, you idiot." Alas, she used the English word. "And you, Sanjay, mind your own business." Another surprise: I hadn't thought they were on a first-name basis. And then, still another surprise: Kriegman came to her rescue.

"Lay off her, Sanjay," he snapped. "Keep your conspiracy theories to yourself and your eyes on the road. No need to discombobulate our poet. He must be thinking we're a nest of vipers." That was true and uninteresting. Rather more interesting was that Thor also used Palermo's first name. "Which, as you should know, Chester," he added unnecessarily, "isn't at all true."

Whether or not that statement was accompanied by a smile I didn't know, as I resolved to keep staring at the road. We had, by the way, slowed down after entering a nameless town with a winding main street lined with private homes, stores, cafés, restaurants, and a church. The effects of the earthquake were visible again: most of the structures displayed very prominent cracks; some of the roofs had caved in; and the church steeple had fallen over, lying in pieces on the sidewalk and street. The damage on the piazza was almost unnoticeable, however, and, as we drove past the throngs assembled around the central fountain, the car slid along the curb and abruptly came to a halt.

"There," said Palermo. "A Chinese restaurant. One can always count on the Chinamen to stay open." He climbed out of the vehicle and we followed. Palermo stretched his arms and did a few preposterous knee bends. "An enterprising people. Did you notice that there's a Chinese restaurant in every town of the world?"

"I could eat a horse." Louise headed for the gaudily decorated entrance guarded on both sides by two weather-beaten green beasts resembling tigers.

Inside, the walls were covered with red-velvet wallpaper (again!) featuring golden dragons and waterfalls. Huge white paper lanterns were suspended from the golden ceiling. Bundles of bamboo that brought to mind Mussolini's *fasci* were arranged along the wall to the right. Surprisingly, the place was empty. The girl at the cash register curtsied and said, "*Bon gio'no.*"

"*Bon giorno,*" Palermo replied. "*Cinque.* Do you speak English?"

"*Si,*" she said with eyes lowered demurely, "but not vely good. Prease forrow me." She led us to a round table near the back. "This goo'?"

"This good."

"He' a' menus."

"*Grazie.*"

"*Plego,*" she answered and melted away.

"What should we order?" It was Kriegman. "Perhaps one of each—meat, noodles, fish, vegetarian, and some special?" The ensuing negotiation, like a bad play by Pinter, went nowhere with a vengeance.

Babylon: "I want shrimp."

Heldenplatz: "I'm allergic to shrimp."

Palermo: "Thor, you choose."

Babylon: "But I want shrimp. You can choose whatever you like, but I want shrimp."

Kriegman: "I can only choose if I have the mandate to choose."

Milosz: "Who wants appetizers?"

Heldenplatz: "As long as there are no shrimp or shellfish."

Babylon: "Well, boys, you can do whatever you like, but I'm ordering the shrimp."

Palermo: "Thor, you choose any four dishes. And you, Mister Milosz, choose the appetizers."

Babylon: "As long as I get my shrimp."

The waitress returned and Thor, Louise, and I placed our orders. She listened intently, scribbled something in her pad, and then giggled shyly: "No ha' wha' you wa'. Solly. Ha' onry Chow Mein."

"Shrimp Chow Mein?" Louise asked.

"No, vely solly, onry legula' Chow Mein, wi' veg'table."

"Then bring us five Chow Mein," I said. "And tea."

"Tea we ha'. OK, fi' veg'table Chow Mein an' tea. Yes?"

"Yes."

The meal was uneventful. Everybody was too hungry to talk and the Chow Mein was surprisingly decent, far better than the swill they served off campus at the Hong Kong Garden. As we sat back contentedly—Louise, who had something stuck between her teeth, kept make infuriating sucking sounds—the waitress brought some sliced oranges and fortune cookies.

"I wonder if they're in English," Thor said and took one, pulling apart the cellophane wrapper and cracking it open. "Indeed!" he exclaimed, his eyebrows rising. "'A big fortune awaits you.' Doesn't it always? What does yours say, Chester?"

"'Keep eyes open. You find inspiration soon.'" Was this another sign of my Muses' return to life?

"Excellent! And quite appropriate for a poet," Thor remarked. "And you, *chère* Louise?"

"'Love is in your future.'"

"And in your past and in your present, I should say," Kriegman smiled maliciously.

"Ee-dee-O!"

"Your turn, Sanjay."

"'Your career will take off.' Well, well—the only question is where."

"Not bad, though nothing to write home about, given your stellar success thus far. Orestes?"

"'Big heart is biggest fortune.'"

"That's no fortune, just a statement, and a stupid one at that," Louise interjected. "I hate it when they do that. Don't they know that fortunes are supposed to be predictive claims?"

"Quite," Kriegman said. "Perhaps we should be going? I suggest we just divide the bill in five. Any objections?"

After quick trips to the restrooms and some photographs in front of the church and its broken steeple, we resumed our journey. We wound our away along the curved mountain roads, but encountered no more devastation. An hour or so later, we passed the Bar-Ristorante Benito where Alberto and I had consumed espressos and conversed with the big Russian. I was going to suggest we stop, but decided that reaching Milano and having a hot shower in some *albergo* should be my priority and said nothing. The traffic was light and we soon saw signs for Malpensa. Palermo turned on the radio and Adriano Celentano's voice exploded on the airwaves.

"Turn it down," Kriegman groaned.

"No, leave it," Louise commanded. "He's divine."

The symmetry of the moment struck me and I suddenly felt truly worthy of the onomatopoeia of the word Thor had applied to me—discombobulated. Celentano had greeted me at the outset of my journey to Caravaggio and Celentano was greeting me at its denouement. I had been in a car and I was now in a car. Were these more signs? Of course they were. And just as I was thinking that a road accident was all that was necessary to make the picture complete, the traffic suddenly thickened and we slowed to a crawl. "I think I see an accident," Palermo said, "just up ahead. We should be past it in a few minutes." The picture *was* complete! The beginning and end had met. Something big *was* in store, of that I was absolutely certain. Where would I encounter it? In Milano, of course: poetic justice demanded that it had to be in Milano, where everything began.

***

Palermo dropped us off at the entrance to Mussolini's imposing train station—*nota bene* that I had used the exact same words to describe the Stazione Centrale when I first arrived in Milano several days ago!—and drove off. Heldenplatz decided to take the night train to Paris and, after inviting all of us to visit him in Argentina, disappeared in the cavernous ticket hall, where I distinctly heard him whistling "Lili Marleen." We checked into one of the overpriced tourist hotels on the square and agreed to meet in an hour in the lobby, which was overrun with the obligatory Japanese tourists filming the faux Futurist paintings lining the walls. Kriegman's room was on the fourth floor, as was Louise's; mine, thank God, was on the second. A large window faced the square and the station; the orange trolley ran just below. The din stood in painful contrast to the quiet of Caravaggio—minus the tremors, of course. The bathtub appeared to be clean enough and, after giving the rusty faucets a mighty twist, the resulting stream of lukewarm water seemed hardly worth the effort. But no matter. I stood with my face beneath the trickle and enjoyed the purification.

So here I was again—in Milano. My flight was due to depart tomorrow afternoon. I'd have time to stroll about the city, take in its animal spirits, and come to my senses. I'd have time enough on the plane or at home to consider what the events of the last week meant. There was no point in over-intellectualizing. My gut would eventually communicate with my mind. Meanwhile, I could have another fine Italian meal and enjoy the lascivious interplay of the orange trolleys and the green trees. You may think my use of the modifier lascivious odd in this context. But no, there was something decidedly erotic about the rush of orange amid the green leaves. Unlike Venice, Florence, and Rome, Milano was bursting with sexuality. Small wonder that the machismo-infused Mussolini felt impelled to construct a train station that aspired to balance the city's innate femininity with his oversized masculinity. Another orange trolley clanged past my window and screeched as it made a slow turn on the square. Even the sounds of the city were erotic. Louise, I decided, would be especially dangerous, especially unhinged in such an environment. I would have to be on my guard. Thank heavens that Kriegman was here as well. I slipped on my jeans, sandals, and a button-down white cotton shirt and took the stairs to the lobby.

The Japanese and their video cameras were still there, though whether it was the same Japanese and the same video cameras as an hour ago I couldn't tell. A group of unmistakable Americans were standing tiredly near the reception desk. Their luggage was piled high on two carts. I looked, but saw no underwear. Three disheveled girls were answering the phones, swiping credit cards, and attempting to smile bravely at the guests. Verily, as Orestes Heldenplatz might have said, it was a hubbub. I picked up a copy of the *International Herald Tribune* from the coffee table. "Massive Earthquake Kills Hundreds, Destroys Towns in Northern Italy," the front-page headline screamed (figuratively, of course). That I knew. What I hadn't known was that the epicenter had been in Caravaggio. Most of the town had been leveled. "'It was hell,' said Samuel Roach, a U.S.-based international consultant in Caravaggio for a gathering of philanthropists. 'My colleagues and I have been doing everything we can to find survivors. I've never seen anything like this.'" Like hell you have, Sammy, I thought. The international community promised to send aid. Rome had mobilized an army unit and planned to rebuild immediately. Fortunately, all the survivors had been rescued. And then, a familiar voice.

"Thor and I have been waiting outside," Louise said sharply. "For twenty minutes. It's too damned crowded in here."

"I was just looking at the paper," I mumbled. "The epicenter was in Caravaggio."

"Imagine that. Come on—*vite*. We're hungry." And then for good measure she added: "*Idiot!*" After all that bad news, my mood improved immediately.

We agreed to view Da Vinci's Last Supper first and then have dinner. Kriegman was sure the painting would still be on display, so we caught a cab and, after coming close to sideswiping several cars, pedestrians, and trolleys—I confess to having been too nervous to have considered the erotic symbolism of bumping up against an orange trolley car—we turned right near the Duomo, navigated some side streets filled with tourists and shoppers, and, after a few more minutes of twisting and turning, pulled up in front of the museum, an unprepossessing building that seemed far too modest for the treasure displayed within it. There was a long line, but Thor flashed his press card and we were ushered in with a bored flick of the guard's wrist and joined the slow-moving procession of art pilgrims. Ten minutes later, we stood behind a barrier in a poorly lit room, some sixty feet away from the painting.

"I can't see anything," Kriegman said. "Can you?"

"Just the bare outlines," I said. "The colors are so dark."

"It hasn't been cleaned."

"But why can't we come closer?" Louise asked. "This is infuriating."

"I can't see a thing. What's the point of looking at it, if you can't see it?"

"Close your eyes and imagine it," I suggested. "Perhaps that's the point."

"That's idiotic," Louise shot back. A guard beckoned to us to move on. A few seconds later we left the room.

"Perhaps it's like that composition by Cage—'Four thirty-three'." I was determined to continue with my thought.

"Never heard of it," Louise said.

"The orchestra sits quietly for four minutes and thirty-three seconds and we're supposed to imagine the sounds."

"Sounds daft to me," Thor said. "What's the point?"

"That way we provide the music."

"Maybe you poets would. We journalists would be writing our next story. Or"—and his eyes sparkled (it may have been the sunlight or his mood)—"composing a sequel: Five thirty-four."

"Sorry, Thor." Louise was actually grinning. "I've already done that one. You'll have to do Five thirty-six."

"The two of you are artistic barbarians!" I couldn't resist smiling.

"*Mais, non, mon ami*: just hungry barbarians."

We decided to walk back to the Duomo. Kriegman suggested we try a fashionable trattoria in the Galleria that journalists liked to frequent. The food was adequate, but the atmosphere might be amusing. It would be expensive, but I didn't object. Louise said she didn't care, as long as we'd have food soon. It was a Friday evening and the streets were crowded with locals and tourists. There was no trace of the *terremoto* and its horrors anywhere. High heels clicked along the sidewalks, throaty laughs rose intermittently from within the cicada-like buzz of the crowds, the honking, screeching, and groaning of impatient automobiles provided rhythmic accompaniment. The cacophony was either a refutation or a demonstration of Cage's composition.

But it was also, I suddenly realized, a continuation of that morning's earthly convulsions. Some ten or twelve hours ago, the earth had roared like a mad lion. Now, here in Milano, it was humanity's turn to out-roar the earth. And it was succeeding. What was this? The assertion of man's will over nature or man's declaration of unity with nature? Or was it nothing—just two instances of mad fury and loud noise that signified nothing at all? I kept my thoughts to myself, sensing that neither of my companions would be sympathetic to my bouts of doubt. These were questions that I would have to answer on my own or, perhaps, with the help of my Muses.

And where were they, my Muses? Had they taken a long hike? Had they been trapped in the debris of Caravaggio? Had they, heaven forbid, boarded the helicopter with Zekovich and were now cavorting with Joe and Dickey? Or were they still with me, here in Milano, amid the cacophonous crowds and thick smells of perfume, sweat, car fumes, and coffee? Time was running out. If they were to return to my side, they would have to do so tonight or tomorrow. Once I adjusted my seatbelt on the plane, this adventure would be over and the creative window of opportunity it represented for me would be closed. Once back on campus, I would come face to face, yet again, with the deadening reality that had driven the Muses away in the first place.

I had never felt quite so invigorated, quite so expectant of a breakthrough, as these last few days at the villa. Had my teaching career become an albatross? Was the routine stifling me? Had the campus become my Przebrzegorzwice? Would I, like Granddad Milosz, have to abandon it? Or should I, like my father Emiliano, simply make a clean break with the past and abandon poetry? If the boo-leet-ZAY defined my past and the Nobel failed to become my guiding light for the future, why should I expect my writer's block ever to melt away? On the other hand, didn't the earthquake signify that my past was dead and destroyed and that a bright future awaited me? If the Muses had been asleep, wouldn't the *terremoto* have awakened them?

***

We reached the Piazza Duomo. Dusk had enveloped the brightly illuminated square and the majestic cathedral. It glowed, seemingly radiating a light of its own. We negotiated the throngs of tourists and souvenir hawkers and finally emerged at the entrance to the Galleria. Kriegman took the lead and, after some searching, found the restaurant in one of the wings. We sat at a small table outside, next to a group of American tourists who were loudly examining the menu and remarking on the outrageously high prices. Thor looked crestfallen, but, after a minute, they rose and left. Their places were immediately taken by several men who had been standing at the bar.

"Jake! Jake Kriegman!" One of them exclaimed. "Well, I'll be! Long time no see!"

"Good to see you, Hilly. Long time no see, indeed. Still covering the financial markets?"

"Is there anything else? And you? Still chasing the skirts?"

"Is there anything else?" Thor turned confidentially toward us. "Hildebrandt Lebkuchen, stringer for the Associated Press. Has been here for ages. The markets—that's about all he's good for."

"Any more news on the quake, Hilly?" I asked. "Chester Milosz," I added and extended my hand. "The Nobel Prize-winning poet."

"No, not that I know of. The markets have been quiet today."

"I meant the earthquake."

"Some minor rumble up in the mountains, I heard. Are you heading out there? I wouldn't worry if I were you." He appeared to be thinking. "So you're a poet? Does that bring home the bacon?"

"We just came from there," I corrected him. "As to the bacon, sure, why not? Depends on how much you eat, I suppose."

"Well, words are words, I reckon." He began thinking again.

"Good to have met you, Hilly," I said peremptorily and opened the sticky menu. "I think I'll have a cheeseburger, fries, and Coke."

"Spaghetti and meatballs for me. Or maybe the pasta puttanesca?"

"Why so modest, boys? I'm going for the Porterhouse: medium rare, Pittsburgh style."

"Living high on the hog, eh, Louise? So utterly indifferent to the potential poundage? By the way, I doubt they'll know what Pittsburgh style is. But it's your call, my sweet. As far as I'm concerned, the pasta is safe. And the burgers are quite decent. See? Who said the universe isn't flat?"

"Tell me, Louise." I decided to change the subject. If La Babylon were lulled by fatigue and hunger, she just might be inclined to answer truthfully. "What did Palermo mean when he said you know better than any of us? Know what better? Come, Louise, truth or dare. You're among friends. Fess up."

"Should I tell him, my sweet?" Thor was positively leering and his usually self-controlled face suddenly resembled that of a porn peddler. "Or will you?"

"Go ahead, my love," she answered icily. (In contrast to what you'd find in cheap novels, I felt no chill running down my spine and had no desire to say, "Brrr.") "But remember: loose lips sink ships. You sink mine, darling, and I sink yours. *Quid* always results in *quo*. Actions always have consequences. So truth or dare, my love?"

"What *are* you two talking about?" I cried, adopting an affected pose of puzzlement verging on annoyance. "I asked a simple question—nothing more. Can't you give me a simple answer?" I was being insincere, of course, as the question and the answer were anything but simple. The situation obviously called for a parenthetical comment, but I suddenly realized that I was bored—utterly, completely, absolutely bored—with parentheses and the meretricious sentiments they embraced. Enough! Enough! Enough! No more hiding from the Muses behind parentheses. Henceforth, I would welcome them into my open arms with colons, commas, and exclamation points!

"Our poet wants a simple answer, Louise—or so he says so. But we can't accommodate him, can we? After all, my dear friend, no answer, not even the simplest, is ever simple, is it? The universe may be flat, but humanity is not. Isn't that right, Louise? The surface always hides many layers of reality—of complexity. What you see is, alas, rarely what you get. As in your poetry, I dare say. Meanings are multiple, words are opaque. The simpler, the worse, I should say."

He had a point. "You're being Delphic, Thor." I said with all the feigned exasperation I could muster. So much feigning was getting to be a chore and a bore. "I need to wash my hands. Where's the men's room?" He pointed to the bar. "I'll be back in a minute. By the way, I've been meaning to ask you: why does no one call you Jake?"

A broad smile expanded along his face: "I'll tell you when you get back."

Louise's eyes rolled and were accompanied by a prolonged groan. "Not another deadly story," she sighed. "Heaven help us all."

***

I was about to step into the bar when I caught a glimpse of the majestic Duomo to my right. It glowed like sugar and its roof was covered with moving stick figures: people! I wouldn't have a chance to return tomorrow, so I hurried across the street, just barely sidestepping one of the orange trolleys that had caught my fancy, and pushed my way through the throngs to the doors of the cathedral. Thor and Louise and the cheeseburger could wait. This time, I had the requisite change and, after bestowing an oily smile on the mustachioed guard, slid through the turnstile and headed toward the staircase that led to the top. It was winding and narrow and could barely accommodate two persons across. A steady stream came downwards and, every time there was a gap in the flow, I rushed to pass the people in front of me. After much jostling, quite out of breath, and with a madly pounding heart, I finally reached the top and followed the narrow pathway along the sloped roofs to the edge of the Duomo. The sugary spires and turrets reached into the dark sky and below, spread out before me like a resplendent valley, lay the vibrant square and the pulsating multitudes. Farther, beyond the square, was a darkness that twinkled with a thousand winking lights and from within that darkness came the clanging of an orange trolley. The view was dazzling. *This was ardor,* I thought, suddenly realizing that my journey to and from Ardor Haus had reached its climax.

"Wow," I heard a girlish voice say, "this beats Disneyland fer shure!"

"My cell doesn't work up here," another one said with the same nasal intonation. "Shoot! I promised to call my mom. She'll kill me if I don't."

Three blondes, very visibly American and in their early twenties, had approached the railing next to me. They wore T-shirts, shorts, and sandals and were chewing gum and whispering and giggling. One of them had dyed the left side of her hair lime green. Another had pierced her nose with two golden rings. The third had elaborate eyelashes that resembled huge fluttering moths. Marlene Dietrich's famous line comparing love-struck men to flame-driven moths—*"Männer umschwirr'n mich, wie Motten um das Licht"*—fluttered through my mind. College students, I thought. I had seen thousands like them. And their casual demeanor suggested they were from California—probably southern California. Were they Valley Girls-turned-coeds? Probably. No, certainly—fer shure.

"Hey, mister," the one with lime-green hair said. "Could you take a pi'ture of us?"

"Sure."

"Thanks," she said and handed me a pink cell phone. "You're American, aren't you?"

"Yes. How did you know?"

"You look it," the one with the nose rings said. "What's your name?"

"Chester Milosz."

"What?!" the green one with the cell phone exclaimed. "The poet? You're the freakin' poet?! We read you in world lit class. No way!"

"The one and only," I said somewhat sheepishly. "And what are your names, ladies?"

"Ada. Hi."

"Lolita. Pleased to meet you."

I could barely contain myself. "Let me guess," I turned to the one with the eyelashes. "You must be Anna Karenina?"

"Hey, wasn't she the actress who starred in those GO-dar films we saw in film class?" one of the others remarked.

"That's go-DAR, silly," eyelashes said. Then she deftly removed the gum with her left hand and floated her right to shake mine.

"Hi-yah, Mister MEE-losh," she meowed. "I'm Musetta and I *really* love your stuff!"

END

OTHER
ANAPHORA LITERARY
PRESS TITLES

PLJ: Interviews with Gene Ambaum and Corban Addison: VII:3, Fall 2015
Editor: Anna Faktorovich

Architecture of Being
By: Bruce Colbert

The Encyclopedic Philosophy of Michel Serres
By: Keith Moser

Forever Gentleman
By: Roland Colton

Janet Yellen
By: Marie Bussing-Burks

Diseases, Disorders, and Diagnoses of Historical Individuals
By: William J. Maloney

Armageddon at Maidan
By: Vasyl Baziv

Vovochka
By: Alexander J. Motyl

CPSIA information can be obtained
at www.ICGtesting.com
Printed in the USA
FFOW04n0134140416
23094FF

9 781681 14243